HER BILLIONAIRE BENEFACTOR

EASTER IN GILEAD

ELIZABETH MADDREY

1

WENDY

I shut my office door and moved around behind my desk. I took a deep breath and lowered slowly into my chair. The silence in the room, the whole office, was comforting. Quiet, like the ancient sick-day quilt—ostensibly made by my grandfather—lay heavily across my shoulders, wrapping me up and offering a thick, almost squishy defense against the world around me.

I glanced down at the blotter-sized calendar on my desk, grateful I'd thought ahead and changed it to the new year before Christmas break.

Christmas.

My mind shied away, but not before the memory of shattering glass, screams, and disorientation as the car flipped twice, made itself known.

"No." My hand flew to my mouth as my voice startled the memory away. I closed my eyes and breathed in through my nose and then held that breath as I focused on counting to eight as slowly as I could, before counting the air back out. Breath control was about the only useful thing I'd gotten out of the last year of therapy.

Oh, sure. The therapist said I was doing great. My parents said I was doing amazingly well. Even my sister—when she, her husband, and their nephew-slash-son had come out—thought I was some kind of walking miracle. But I knew the truth.

I was good at pretending.

I pressed my fingers to my eyes. "Stop, Wendy. Just stop. That's not why you're here."

With a decisive nod, I glanced quickly at the door—still shut —and moved to turn on my computer. Maybe talking to myself aloud was a new coping mechanism, but it wasn't as if I was the only person in the world who did it. And I didn't have whole conversations.

Mostly.

Fingers on the keyboard, I logged in. While the operating system did its thing, I glanced at the calendar again. January first. Another new year. Another go-round with the Easter passion play here at the college. Another chance for me to approach alumni, and others, with my hand out to ensure our endowment remained robust.

Mom and Dad said this was a new start. Time to move on and get my feet back under me. As if I was ever going to date again. Marry. Have a new family.

I snorted.

Like I'd risk that.

"Enough." I opened my email and smiled. Three hundred messages. That ought to fill the afternoon. I'd gone to church with my parents because it was expected, but begged off lunch and an afternoon in their living room while they tried to pretend everything was normal and I acted as though I was absolutely, one hundred percent healed so it would make them feel better. They hadn't argued.

I think Mom suspected I'd end up here. My office was more of a home than my house. I'd slept on my couch too many nights to tell, when the idea of going back to the house had been unbearable. Thankfully, Mom hadn't said anything. I didn't want to add more lies to the words that clouded the air between us.

I started at the top, clicking the email, skimming the contents, and then deleting or filing it, depending on its importance.

Click. Skim. Delete.

Click. Skim. Delete.

It was a calming rhythm that I sank into.

The desk phone jarred me out of my email trance.

I glanced over and frowned at the area code. It wasn't local. It was...I scrunched my forehead...Chicago?

Even as I tried to figure who I might know in Chicago and considered ignoring the call—they had to be expecting to leave a voice mail, right?—I reached over and answered on autopilot.

"Wendy Hall."

There was silence for a moment—just long enough for me to wonder if the caller had given up—then a man spoke. "Oh. Hi. I was expecting voice mail."

I didn't know how to answer that. "Duh" was probably the wrong way to go, but it was all I could come up with. I tried to inject a smile in my word. "How can I help you?"

"My name is Preston Swift. I'm interested in speaking to someone about partnering with the college financially."

"I'd be happy to help you with that. I'm the head of development here at the college." I was, in fact, the only employee dedicated to development, but that didn't sound nearly as impressive as saying I was the head. Fundraising was at least as much about optics as anything else. "If I could get your address, I'd be happy to put a packet in the mail. Once you go over it, we could set up a time to have a video call. Or, better, if you're able to make a visit, we could talk in person and I could show you around the campus."

"I can come down. Would this week be too soon?"

My eyebrows lifted, but I quickly switched over to the electronic calendar that held all the administration schedules. Students would be returning to campus from their break starting on Wednesday. Classes started back up next Monday. And that was the kickoff for audition week for the passion play, as well. "No, that would be fine. How long do you think you'll stay?"

He sighed. "I don't know. My great-grandmother is pushing for this. She and Great-grandpa met at the college and now that she's approaching ninety-five, she's decided it's time to do something to say thank you."

I smiled slightly. "What a lovely story. Swift, you said?"

"It's my mother's grandmother. So you'd want to look for Coulter. And Cross. Great-grandpa was a Cross." He cleared his throat. "I assume you're verifying my story?"

"Not so much verifying. We don't actually require a connection with the college if people want to give us money."

He laughed.

I winced. That had probably come out less tactfully than it should have.

"GG would like you."

It took me a minute to realize GG was what he called his great-grandmother. "Thanks."

"Let me talk to her and see what she wants me to do. When I look on the map, it shows an airport in town?"

"Sure. But you're not going to find major airlines coming in and out. There are a handful of hoppers that fly over from Wichita, but you're almost always better off driving. If you don't mind renting a car. Or we can have someone come over and pick you up."

"I have a plane."

Oh. My heart went pitter pat as I considered the financial

partnership opportunities with someone who had their own plane. That could be major. Maybe even provide me enough leverage with the college president to hire myself an admin. There was enough busy work and paperwork that went with my position, that having someone to help—even part time—would be huge. "Great. Then yes, the airport isn't far. If you let me know when you're arriving, I can make sure someone picks you up."

"Can I just rent a car?"

I didn't stop the snicker fully before it came out, but I made an effort to turn it into a cough. "Sorry. There aren't a lot of car rental options in Gilead. You could call the companies at the Wichita airport and see if they'd drive something over for you."

"I might do that. I'll let you know."

"Of course." My pen hovered over the blank scratch pad I'd dragged near, hoping to make notes about his visit. So far, there was nothing to write. "Can I get your email address? I can give you some information electronically, at least, before you arrive. And it'll make it easier to get in touch about your visit."

"Sure. It's p-r-e-s at Preston Swift dot com."

I scribbled it down and circled it. I still didn't have a lot to go on in terms of researching the guy, but I knew how to dig. It was part of my job to understand potential donors and know how to hook them. "Perfect. Thanks. I'll send that email now and look forward to hearing back when you've firmed up your dates for a visit. I can include hotel information in the packet, if you'd like."

"Yeah, that sounds great. Appreciate your time."

"It's my pleasure. Have a good afternoon."

"Uh-huh. You too. Bye."

I shook my head and hung up the phone before turning back to the computer. There was still quite a bit of email that needed to be gone through, but for now, I wanted to know more about this mysterious potential donor and what I should expect.

First, though, I opened a new email, typed in his information at the top, and copied in our standard "Thanks for your interest in supporting Gilead Bible College" cover letter before attaching the pdf versions of several of our brochures.

I hit send and mentally checked that off my list.

Now? To see what I could dig up.

Time ticked by as I followed links from one news article to another collecting information about Preston Swift and the Swift family. Did he say "of the Chicago Swifts?" He could. That much was obvious. His family went back to the early 1800s and played a large part in establishing the meatpacking industry there. They'd moved into more general food service in the last fifty or so years.

We didn't have royalty in America, but families like his came close. Maybe he wasn't a Vanderbilt, but he wasn't far off. From everything I could tell, the family had held on to their fortune and made it grow.

I pushed back from the computer and rolled my head on my shoulders. If he wanted to bring some of their billions—that's right, with a "b"—to the college, I was definitely not saying no.

I briefly wondered if my brother-in-law Scott knew Preston, but almost as quickly as I had the thought, I dismissed it. Scott's billions were a fairly recent thing. Like in-the-last-two-years recent. It didn't seem likely that old money like the Swifts had was going to mix and mingle with the modern-day upstarts.

I chuckled to myself.

It was entirely possible that Preston wasn't going to end up being as snooty as I was anticipating. On the other hand? I had good reason to know that men—especially rich men—were good at hiding their true nature if it suited them.

"Stop it." I hissed under my breath and scooted back to the computer. Time to finish up with the email and then go home.

I closed my eyes and swallowed the lump in my throat.

I didn't want to go home. I could crash here on the couch. Again. But I had a sneaking suspicion my mom was going to "happen to be in the neighborhood" this evening. If I wasn't home?

I shook my head. It didn't bear thinking about.

In the fall, Mom and Dad had cut a trip to the Caymans short because I'd been dodging their calls. I appreciated their concern. I really did.

It was also smothering.

I was trying to move on. Move past things. Start over. Or something. New year, new me. Wasn't that what all the magazines claimed women should get excited for as January dawned?

I forced myself back to my computer to finish up getting through the emails. I'd swing by the grocery store on my way home and get a container of soup from the deli and a fresh loaf of bread from the bakery department. That would handle dinner. And probably lunch for tomorrow, at least. And if Mom did swing by, she'd see that I was eating.

Everyone won.

At this point in my life, I was going to take whatever wins I could find.

2

PRESTON

What kind of ridiculous backwater didn't have a rental car place?

I scowled at my laptop before setting it next to me on the couch and pushing up to pace around the living room. This whole thing was ridiculous.

I strode over to the window and looked out at the rooftop garden, now covered in a thin layer of snow. It was tempting to step outside and look out over Lake Michigan, but I knew from experience that the winter wind whipped across the penthouse balcony colder and icier than anyone expected. It didn't always stop me, but today I was still dressed for church, not for wandering around in the Chicago winter, and I didn't feel like changing.

Why had the woman been working on a Sunday afternoon?

I tucked my hands in my pockets and wandered through the main floor of the massive penthouse I called home. It was technically my grandmother's place, and it reflected her tastes more than my own. It might be more accurate to say it reflected the tastes of Grandmother's designer, who'd been bucking for a feature in *Architectural Digest*. The problem, of course, was that our family was rich but not famous. So no one particularly cared to see how we lived. But once the money had been spent, Grandmother wasn't redoing things simply because she'd ended up with a reasonably unlivable space. Oh, no. She talked Mom into moving in together in a more modest home in Buena Park. Grandmother took the coach house and Mom had the main. And then, I'd gotten the whole spiel about how we shouldn't let this place sit empty and before I knew what hit me, I'd sold my comfortable, modern condo and moved into this gilded marble monstrosity.

I did love the views.

Of course, GG had laughed herself into a coughing fit when I'd visited her in the retirement home where she lived and told her the whole story. I suspected she'd already known all of it. She and Mom were close. Mom wanted to bring her to live at the house, but GG wouldn't hear of it. She needed too much care at her age, and she didn't want Mom to deal with it. Or so she said.

I suspected she enjoyed being away from Grandmother more than anything. Mom's grandma and Dad's mom had never really gotten along. GG didn't approve of Dad's family money. Grandmother considered the money an integral part of her identity.

In the kitchen, I got a loaf of bread out of the cupboard and studied the contents of the refrigerator before dragging out a container of sliced roast beef and two individually wrapped cheese slices.

"Yo. Pres? You here?"

"In the kitchen." The other joy of living in the family home was that everyone felt perfectly comfortable just coming in. And I really couldn't say anything about it. Mostly I didn't mind, but sometimes it got old.

"Hey, man."

"Coop." I squirted mayo on two slices of bread and started layering on roast beef. "Want a sandwich?"

"Sure. No mayo. I don't know how you eat that." Cooper stuck out his tongue. "Got mustard?"

"Probably." I got out more bread and set it aside before peeling open the cheese slices. "What brings you by?"

"Can't a guy just want to see his brother?"

I glanced over, eyebrows raised. "Sure. But I thought you had a hot date last night. I'm honestly surprised you're even out of bed yet."

Cooper shrugged and opened the fridge. He rummaged around until he pulled out a bottle of Dijon. He shook the bottle, then squirted it on the bread I'd set out for him. "We didn't even make it to midnight. She was just...ugh."

I snickered. "That's an accurate summary of my feelings on her. What was her name? Sandra?"

"No. Sandra was in the summer. This was Melanie." Cooper frowned. "You make it sound like I'm some kind of rich playboy."

I bit my tongue and slid the roast beef over so he could add what he wanted. "There's cheese in the fridge."

"Just the singles, right?"

"Why mess with a classic?"

"Maybe because you can't tell from the taste if you've remembered to remove the wrapper?" Cooper sighed and flipped the top piece of bread onto his sandwich. "How did you grow up in the same house I did and eat like this?"

"Maybe this is how I rebel." It wasn't too far off. We'd always had a cook growing up, so there were no hurried frozen dinners on our way from school to soccer practice. And a drive-through? Never. I crossed the kitchen and got down two plates. "Might as well be civilized."

Cooper scoffed. "Why start now?"

I flashed a grin, dropped my sandwich on my plate, and headed into the dining room. I pulled out one of the vaguely baroque chairs and sat.

"I don't know how you eat in here." Cooper shook his head as he pulled out the chair across from me. "Why don't you redecorate?"

I shrugged. "I'm hoping not to have to live here forever. Mostly I pretend it's a hotel."

Cooper looked around. "That works, actually. Ritzy and high end. Not bad."

I grinned. "You praying or am I?"

"I can." Cooper folded his hands and closed his eyes.

I'd barely managed the same before he dove in.

"Thanks, God, for the food. Even if it's just American singles because my brother doesn't know what real cheese is. Help it not to kill us so we can serve You daily. Amen."

I shook my head. "You don't have to eat here. You know that, right? In fact, I'm pretty sure you own a really great condo with its own lake views. And a more streamlined, modern sense of style."

"Now that you've got the whole hotel thing going in my head though, I might never leave."

"Oh, no. Nope. There's no maid service here. No turndown service either. And if I'm going to leave something on your pillow before bedtime, you're going to want to think twice before you eat it."

Cooper laughed hard enough that he had to set down his sandwich.

"Glad to amuse." I picked up half of my sandwich and bit in. "But really, what brings you here?"

"A guy can't just drop in on his brother?"

I studied Cooper as I chewed. After I swallowed, I started to reach for a drink then realized I hadn't grabbed one. I pushed back my chair and stood. "Pop?"

"Yeah. Thanks." Cooper picked up his sandwich.

I gave him one more long look before heading into the kitchen. I grabbed two pops out of the fridge and took them back to the dining room. I slid one across the table to Cooper. "Here. Now spill."

"You hate the rug in here that much?" Cooper popped the top on his can.

"You're a laugh riot." I opened my can and took a drink before picking up my sandwich again.

Cooper sighed. "I don't know. I guess I didn't want to start the new year alone. Mom's busy. So is Grandma. The rest of the guys are doing their annual movie marathon, but they chose Marvel and I just wasn't feeling it. Figured you'd skip, too."

"Yeah, the invite Grayson texted basically said I was welcome but they knew I wouldn't come." I reached for my drink. "I mean, he wasn't wrong. What's Mom doing?"

"She got it in her head that she's going to start quilting. She's doing an online workshop on the basics."

My eyebrows lifted. "Quilting? Mom?"

"Exactly. But whatever."

I couldn't see it. Mom had never been crafty. She was happy to toss things when they got ripped—even if it caused emotional trauma to lose a favored stuffed animal rather than having it repaired. "Are we sure she's feeling all right?"

Cooper chuckled. "She gave me the look when I asked her that. Now, she's doubling down. She said something about showing us all."

"Oh, man." When Mom made up her mind like that, there was no quitting. "I guess we'll be getting quilted stuff for gifts until she figures she's made her point."

"That'll look amazing in here."

I snickered at the sarcasm dripping off his words. Quilted anything with the overly baroque and gilt madness left by the decorator was going to be a look. "You wanna do our own movie marathon?"

"Yeah. Why not? Can we do something with spies?"

"Bond?" There were too many for us to even consider trying to get them all. "Choose an actor."

"Let's stick with Craig."

Not my favorite, but I could roll with it. He was more of a street fighter than the suave hero I associated with the role, but the movies were still fun. "All right. In between, maybe you can help me figure out what I'm looking for when I go visit this college in Kansas."

"You're really doing that?"

"GG doesn't ask for much. It feels like something easy to do for her."

Cooper nodded and stuffed the last bite of his sandwich into his mouth.

"You want to come along?"

His eyebrow lifted. "To Kansas? In January? No. I have zero desire to do that. You're the one that said yes to GG. Sounds like it's all you."

"Figured." I finished my sandwich and stood. "Grab your dishes and let's go."

Cooper collected his stuff and started toward the kitchen.

Kansas in January wasn't really high on my list, either. But it was GG.

3

WENDY

I held the door for the group of chattering college students who were exiting Heavenly Brew as I arrived. The scent of coffee hit me as I stepped in. I didn't always splurge on the coffee shop. I had a fancy machine at home—Mark had insisted it was a good investment and then claimed it was too hard to use. So I'd figured it out. But it was a lot of work for one person and I was tempted to get one of those pod machines and just call it a day. I drank coffee because I was addicted to caffeine, not because I loved the taste and made it part of my identity.

"Morning, Letty. Bet you're glad the students are back." I stepped up to the counter and eyed the menu.

"Definitely. What can I get you?"

"I'll go with the peppermint mocha."

Letty smiled as she pressed buttons on the cash register. "Can't get enough of the Christmas season, huh?"

"Something like that." I just liked peppermint and I knew it was going away before too much longer. I checked the total and handed her my credit card.

"They'll probably go away until next Christmas season after

the weekend, so it's good you're getting it now." She handed back my card. "You want your receipt?"

"No, thanks."

"I'll get that going for you."

I slid down the counter toward the pickup area while Letty busied herself making my order.

"Hi, Ms. Hall."

I turned, smiling as I spotted the girl behind me. "Hi, Kara. Did you have a good break?"

"Yeah. It's a lot warmer in Florida. And less wind." She shrugged. "But I'm looking forward to this semester."

"You graduate in May, right?"

She nodded.

"What's next?" I could have kicked myself for asking. I'd hated it when I was pressed like that going into my senior year. Most people had an idea. Some kind of goal. But not everyone. And for those who didn't, the questions were probably super annoying.

"I have a standing offer at the place where I've worked during summers, but I thought I might try to line up some other interviews during spring break. I guess we'll see." Kara tipped her head to the side. "When are auditions for the play?"

"Next week. You trying out?"

Kara shook her head. "Oh. No. Not me. My roomie keeps talking about it though. I thought I'd try to be there for moral support. Depending on her time slot, I guess."

"Will you be an extra in the crowd scenes? Or help backstage?"

She wrinkled her nose. "It's not really my thing. My folks might come up for one of the performances. They've never been and they're acting like this is their last chance."

I chuckled. "Well, let me know and I'll get you a backstage tour if you think they'd enjoy that."

"I will. Thanks."

"Wendy, your mocha's ready." Letty set a cup on the counter.

"Nice to see you, Kara. Will you be working in the office again this semester?"

"I think so."

I reached for my coffee and raised it in a little salute. "I'll see you around, then."

My phone rang as I pushed open the coffee shop door and stepped out into the cold breeze. I fumbled it out of my purse and frowned. I accepted the call and tried to inject cheer into my voice. "Hi, Mom."

"Morning, baby. How are you today?"

"Great. You?" So far, this conversation was traveling down the same script we always covered.

"Just fine. Dad and I were wondering if you needed any help with anything this weekend."

I hurried to my car and climbed in behind the wheel, grateful to be out of the wind. "I don't think so."

"You're set for auditions next week?"

"I assume so." I sipped my mocha and closed my eyes. "It's not like I have a huge role here, Mom. I sit in on the auditions, sure, but I don't make decisions. In fact, I might not be able to sit in this year anyway. We have a big potential donor coming in on Sunday night. I'll need to escort him around and make sure he gets a good sense of things here."

"That's nice. How long is he staying?"

"Not sure. He didn't seem to know. He'd planned to come down this week, but the blizzard threw him off and he decided to wait. I can't imagine he'll be here more than a couple of days though." It wasn't as if we were a huge school. I could give a reasonably complete tour of the campus in under an hour. Two if we went through every building. But I wasn't going to tell someone with the kind of money Preston Swift had how long they could stay.

"Oh. Well. That's good for the school."

"Hope so. I'm going to spend a little more time in the archives today looking for information on the guy's great-grandparents. They're why he's coming."

"What if I met you there at lunch? I could bring chicken Caesars."

I started the engine. "How about I let you know? I'm not sure what the morning is going to be like until I get in and look at the computer."

"Oh." Disappointment laced Mom's words.

I winced. Should I take back the words? They were true. But also, I just didn't want to commit. Mom would want to talk about how I was feeling and she wasn't going to be satisfied with generic responses.

"Well. Let me know, okay? The salads are easy to throw together if you can make it work."

"Of course. Thanks, Mom."

"You know I love you, right?"

"I do, Mom. I love you, too."

"All right. I'll talk to you later. Hopefully see you at lunch. Bye now."

I ended the call and didn't bother to sigh. I wanted to be grateful for her concern. And for her love. But sometimes it was smothering. Mark had never liked how close I was to my parents. I'd pulled back to make him happy. Now it was habit.

"Am I supposed to change that, Jesus? Because I just don't know." I waited a minute to see if I'd get some kind of supernatural response. When I didn't, I checked my mirrors and pulled away from the curb.

It was a short drive to the school. Campus was coming back to life after the Christmas break. Students were hurrying between buildings, wrapped up against the wind and the chill. Classes didn't start until Monday, but the majority of students came as soon as the dorms reopened. We had a close-knit student body, and nearly all of them did something with the passion play that we put on every spring. Those who wanted a speaking part were working on their auditions. The folks who would work on sets and behind the scenes were busy thinking about what needed to be done before the first performance.

And of course there were the overachievers who were already in the library getting a jump on their assignments.

I smiled slightly as I parked and cut the engine in front of the administration building. I didn't have a lot to do with the students as part of my job. I sat on the admission committee and had a say in some of the scholarships, but that was still behind the scenes. Even so, we were small enough that I learned a lot of names and recognized even more faces.

I made my way up the path to the main door and in.

"Good morning, Wendy."

"Morning, Lissa." I nodded to the secretary and started toward my office.

"You've been getting quite a few calls from a Preston Swift."

I stopped and turned. "He called the main number?"

Lissa nodded. "He said he'd left a message on your desk number but hadn't heard back."

"Did he say when he left the message?" Because I didn't have much of a life. There'd been nothing there last night when I left for the day. And it wasn't even nine a.m. yet.

Lissa shook her head. "I guess he's antsy."

"I guess so. I'll call him back first thing. Thanks."

"Anything you want to share with the class?" Lissa wiggled her eyebrows.

My smile was tight. "He's a potential donor, Liss."

"Oh. Well, you can't blame a girl for hoping. He sounds cute."

"How does someone sound—you know what, never mind. I don't think I want to know what that means. Have a good one." I waved and headed to my office.

I took the time to hang up my coat and get organized for the day. Preston Swift had waited this long, he could wait a little longer. I had thirty minutes before my first meeting. That ought to be plenty of time to deal with whatever problem had necessitated multiple calls.

I picked up the handset and, after a glance at the notepad where I'd written down his number, dialed.

"Preston Swift."

"Good morning, Mr. Swift. This is Wendy Hall returning your call." I winced at the rhyme. I tried to avoid doing that. It had been the one major checkmark in the negative column of taking back my maiden name. But the positives had definitely outweighed any objections.

"Call me Preston, please."

"Mm. How can I help you?"

"I'm changing my plans and will be flying in this afternoon. My great-grandmother isn't doing well. She fell Monday night and with her age...I told her I'd hurry. She really wants to know this is taken care of before she goes to Jesus."

"I'm sorry to hear that. What time will you land? I can pick you up at the airport. I imagine it's too short notice to get a rental driven over."

"It is. And apparently, I can't get into my hotel room until Monday."

"Oh." I tried to figure out why. Parents didn't typically bring students back after Christmas break. Maybe a handful, but not enough to fill the rooms like at graduation or the start of a new year.

"I wondered if you knew of anyone with a guest room I could use. I'm happy to pay, of course. I'd just rather not sleep on the streets." He chuckled.

"And you can't wait until Monday?"

"GG was very pleased when I told her I'd come today."

I closed my eyes and tried to think. I had room, but that would be completely improper. My parents had room, but I definitely wasn't going to subject him to that. "You can stay at my house. I can bunk at my parents'."

"I don't want to put you out."

"It's no problem. They'll be thrilled." I pinched the bridge of my nose, praying it would stave off the headache I felt brewing. "What time should I be at the airport?"

"Around four thirty. It doesn't look like Gilead is huge, and I don't mind waiting. I can just text you when I land."

That would let me do more to get ready. My house was... basically clean. But if someone who was not me was staying there, it was going to need a lot more work polishing things up. "You really don't mind?"

"I wouldn't offer if I did."

I nodded. I was like that, too. "Good to know. That would be helpful."

"Great. I need your cell number."

"Right." I hesitated. I hadn't given my personal contact details to a donor ever. Or to a man in what might as well have been forever. It felt strange. But this was a work-related thing and nothing else. I could have the guy call the main number and have them let me know, but honestly, why would I do that in today's world? This was no big deal. I repeated that to myself in my head a few times before rattling off the number.

Preston read it back to me.

"That's correct."

"Let me just send you a text now. That way you aren't confused when it comes up later."

My eyebrows hiked up. Did he think I had random people texting me all the time? I could assure him that wasn't the case. But also? Why would I bother? He could think what he wanted. My phone sang out the recognizable notes from Beethoven's Ninth as the text came in. I tapped on it and my lips twitched up slightly as I read the note.

"Did you get it?"

"I did. Thanks. I'll save your contact so it shows your name. Then I definitely won't be confused."

He made a noise that might have been a snicker. "All right. I'll see you later this afternoon. I look forward to meeting you in person."

"And you as well. Have a safe flight." He acknowledged my comment and then ended the call. I set my phone down and stared blankly at the wall as the things I needed to do swirled through my mind.

I reached for a notepad and pen so I could organize my thoughts and make a plan. When in doubt, write things down. I'd learned that when I was juggling being the wife Mark expected, being the mother my girls needed, and still having a career I enjoyed.

I pushed away the emotions that tried to well up at the thought of Mark and the girls. Now was not the time, and work was *definitely* not the place.

Make the list. Right.

I wrote the items as they occurred to me: clean the house, call Mom and explain the situation, pack a bag for five days, just to be safe. He'd said he could move to the hotel on Monday, but politeness would dictate I offer him my house for his whole stay.

Kansas might not be the South, but Mom was a stickler for hospitality.

I blew out a breath. I really did not want to move back in with my parents for an extended amount of time. Four days might as well be an eternity.

I shoved that thought away, too, to deal with later.

Or never.

Never was good.

If Preston Swift took me up on the offer, he was going to need to let me come by and collect more clothes. How long was he staying?

Ugh.

Why didn't he know? How hard was it, really, to look around, write a check, and then go home? We had donors who hadn't set foot on the campus in decades who still managed to give us money routinely.

I frowned down at my list and tapped my pen against the notepad. There were probably more items that needed to go on here, but I couldn't—groceries! I added that to the list and searched my brain for more.

It would do for now.

I swiveled to my computer and typed up a quick email to Lissa and the dean. I didn't want them wondering where I was. Since schmoozing potential donors was the biggest part of my job, no one should complain that I was out today, but it was always good to make sure.

I sent the email and picked up my cell. After a deep breath, I tapped on Mom's contact.

"Hi, baby!" The joy in Mom's voice unleashed an avalanche of guilt. "Are we on for salads after all?"

"Actually, I need your help."

"What can I do?"

I hadn't thought it was possible to have more guilt cascade down on me, but there it was. Mom—and Dad—loved me. I knew this. And while yes, a lot of the time it felt like being smothered, it came from a good place. I needed to remember that. I cleared my throat. "A new potential donor is coming in today. He changed his plans, I guess. For some reason, he can't get into the hotel until Monday."

Mom started to laugh. "You didn't listen to the local news today, did you?"

"No?" Why that mattered was beyond me.

"The roof of the men's dorm leaked. Not a lot of damage, but obviously it needs to be repaired. So the guys who were impacted are filling up rooms in the hotel until Sunday night. Maybe longer if the fix can't be finished in time."

"Ah." I glanced at the emails piling up in my inbox and skimmed the subjects. There it was. I clicked on the notice from the facilities team. "I see it, now. Well, that explains it."

"So what's he going to do?"

I sighed. "I offered him my house. Which means I'm hoping I can stay with you and Dad until he can move to the hotel."

"Of course you can." The giddiness in Mom's tone was a little scary. Just what did she have planned?

"I'll be escorting him around the whole time he's here. You might not see much of me." I would make sure of it. Even if Preston decided he wanted to hang out at my place alone, I wasn't going to be sitting around my parents' house twiddling my thumbs. I could hide in my office, if nothing else.

"Of course. Of course. I'll just enjoy having you when you're here. I'll make sure your room's ready."

My room was ready. Mom knew it. I knew it. Mom knew I knew. But whatever.

"I appreciate it. Do you think you could help me straighten up at my place?"

"I'd be happy to. You have all the supplies you need?"

"Yes, Mom. I have cleaning supplies." I might not love cleaning, but Mark had insisted on a sparkling home. "That said, if you wanted to hit the grocery store on your way over, it would save me a trip."

"What should I get?"

How was I supposed to know that? "Just...whatever you think someone would want. I don't know if he cooks, but I'd like him to have the option. I'll obviously offer to take him out, but I imagine he'll at least want breakfast at home. Snacks? Maybe see if they have one of those coffee pod machines and get some pods. I don't think he's going to want to learn to use Mark's monstrosity."

Mom chuckled. "Probably not. Unless he's already a coffee snob and knows how."

"Then he'll be welcome to use it. But I wouldn't want him to have to go without if he needs something first thing." I looked back down at my list. "I'll meet you at my house in an hour?"

"Or thereabouts. I'll go ahead and make those salads. We can have them for lunch while we're cleaning."

"Thanks, Mom."

"It's my pleasure. Love you. See you in a bit."

Mom hung up before I could reply.

I set my phone down and turned back to my work email. At the top was a reply from the dean—he was happy for me to take whatever time I needed and make sure Mr. Swift had a good experience at the college.

I snickered. It wasn't every day we had someone with that kind of family money interested in the school. The dean got it. So did I. This could be huge.

And if it fell through? Well, that could be huge for me. Just not in a good way.

4

PRESTON

I taxied my Cessna off the Gilead runway to the parking area. Landing in Kansas had been interesting. Everything was flat. It should have been easy—certainly easier than the time I'd flown with three of my brothers to Catalina Island and had to land on their airstrip that was carved out of the top of a mountain. If you misjudged there, you had to hurry and switch to taking back off before you plummeted off the other side of the island. Here it looked like I could have landed anywhere without much trouble.

Except for the wind.

Chicago was windy. I'd figured I was prepared for landing with wind because of it. But the Kansas wind had a different feel to it.

I couldn't explain more than that without spending time thinking about it, and that seemed pointless.

No one was going to ask. Or care. It was going to be, "How was your flight?" And I'd say, "Good." And that would be the end of it.

Which was as it should be.

I went through the steps to shut down the plane's engine,

then pushed open the door and climbed out. There were still things to do to make sure the plane was secure. I'd expected—somewhat—that there might be people around to help. So far? No one.

It was fine. I'd done it all on my own before and I could do it on my own now.

I made my way around the plane, doing all the little tasks required to keep it from getting damaged. When I was satisfied, I grabbed my suitcase and laptop bag out of the back and locked the doors. Then I took out my phone and texted Wendy Hall.

I headed toward the short, squat building that had to be the main airport. I supposed I should be grateful there was an airport in Gilead, but maybe I would have been better off flying to Wichita and driving after all. At least then I'd have a car.

I picked up my pace as I neared the door. It was chillier than I'd expected. Hopefully, I wouldn't have to wait for her outside.

I pulled on the handle and, *thank You, Jesus*, the door opened. I stepped in out of the cold and stood for a minute, letting the heat soak into me.

My phone dinged.

I fished it out of my pocket. She'd responded with a simple, "Ten minutes."

All right. That wasn't long. I glanced around and spotted some seats pushed up against one of the walls. I sat and scrolled through my email. There wasn't anything major. That was a good thing. The family knew not to bother me when I was flying. Not that I'd had my phone on while I was in the air anyway, but if driving distracted was bad, flying distracted was even worse.

I switched over to my contacts and tapped on GG's entry. It rang four times before she picked up.

"Hello?" Her voice was quiet and wavery. She sounded frail.

And old. And while I knew she was both of those things, hearing it in her voice was new.

"Hi, GG. It's Pres. I'm in Gilead."

"Oh, honey. I'm glad. Thank you."

"It's no trouble."

"What do you think of it?" Her question ended in a wheeze. Quiet murmurs filled the background and I pictured her nurse fussing over her—probably suggesting she shouldn't talk. GG was stubborn.

"It's flatter than I thought possible."

GG chuckled. Then coughed, wet and thick.

"I won't keep you. You rest. I'll email pictures though, so make sure Carrie shows you, okay?"

"Okay. Love you."

"I love you, too, GG." I ended the call and closed my eyes. She'd gone from a feisty woman I'd believed would live forever to someone I worried wouldn't live long enough for me to make it home. Especially since I didn't know when I'd get home. GG had given me a list of things I needed to do while I was here in Gilead, and there was no going home until it was complete.

The endowment would happen regardless.

So why had GG insisted I come here? I couldn't answer that question. GG was the only one who knew her reasons, and she wasn't telling.

I checked the time, then stood. I'd visit the washroom and then head out front. No reason to make Wendy park and come in when I was perfectly capable of meeting her.

It was warmer in the front of the building. I dug my sunglasses out of my laptop bag and slid them on. I could see a car heading this direction. Whether or not it was my ride remained to be seen, but no one was sneaking up on anyone in Kansas.

A few minutes passed while I watched the car approach. The

driver stopped dutifully at the sign, even though it was clear there was no one coming, then pulled into the circle in front of the airport.

The woman behind the wheel was pushing open her door before I stepped down off the curb.

"Hi. You must be Mr. Swift. I'm Wendy Hall. It's good to meet you." She spoke as she hurried around the car. She extended her hand with a harried smile.

I took her hand, surprised at its warmth and the strength of her grip. "Preston. Please."

"Right. You said that. You can call me Wendy. Let me get your bag."

"I've got it." I grabbed the handle of my roller bag and started toward the rear of her SUV.

Wendy hurried ahead of me and opened the tailgate.

The inside of the car was spotless. The carpet in the back showed signs of recent vacuuming. I lifted my suitcase in and slid my laptop bag beside it. "I feel bad messing up your carpet lines."

The pink of her cheeks darkened. "Don't worry about it. I can always make more."

I chuckled and reached up to close the trunk.

Wendy had done the same and her hand brushed mine. She jerked away and took a step back.

Interesting.

I closed the trunk and put my hands in my pockets.

"Do you want to go straight to the house or shall I give you a campus tour and show you around town?"

"A tour sounds great." I looked around before heading toward the passenger seat. How long would a tour actually take? Ten minutes? Fifteen?

Why had GG insisted I needed to be here in person?

I climbed in, closed the door, and reached for my seatbelt.

Wendy slid behind the wheel and glanced over at the airport building. "Do we need to wait?"

"What would we be waiting for?"

She frowned slightly, making little creases in her forehead. "Your pilot? Or pilots? I don't know a lot about private planes, but I assume they need someone to fly them."

I grinned and tapped my chest. "You're looking at him."

"Oh." Puzzlement flashed on her face before she schooled her expression and shifted into Drive. "Then we'll get on with the tour. This is the airport."

I chuckled. "I guess it's not a bustling hub."

"Not usually. We get some charters in during the passion play every spring. There are some families who fly in with their kids at the start of the school year. And we have a handful of families who live out here who commute by plane to Wichita." She shrugged.

I nodded.

Wendy pointed the car toward the rise of buildings in the distance and began to drive. "I thought we could go through town first and then over to the college. Although, if you want to get settled at my house and take some time to relax, we can do that."

"I'd love to see the college." I glanced over. Was she trying to get rid of me? Or was I reading more into her words than was there. "I don't mean to interrupt your day though, if you have things you need to be doing. You can drop me on campus and I can walk around."

"Oh. No. I'm sorry if I gave you that impression. I just know after I've traveled, I usually need a minute."

Okay. That made sense. And if I'd come a long way, I could see that being the case. "It's only about a two-hour flight. I appreciate your thoughtfulness."

Wendy's smile didn't reach her eyes. "This is our main street.

Heavenly Brew is a fantastic coffee shop. Letty is the woman who runs it. She also provides some of the concessions for the passion play."

I angled in my seat so I could see Wendy when I spoke. "Tell me more about the passion play. GG mentioned it. I did a little online sleuthing, but I still don't really get it."

"A passion play is basically an Easter play. It covers the passion of Christ—the time from His triumphal entry into Jerusalem, through his trial, crucifixion, and resurrection."

"Okay. My church does a big cantata every Easter. It's like that?" Didn't most churches do something like this at Easter? What was the big deal?

"Similar. Except we have live animals and more actors and it's generally a larger scale than what your average church puts on. There are some famous passion plays around the world—Germany probably has the most famous, but there's one in the Badlands of Canada as well. And ours is pretty well known here in the states. At least amongst people who look for this sort of thing." Wendy shrugged.

"I don't mean to be offensive." I looked out the window at the quaint town. College-aged kids wandered among the shops. "Did you mention classes start back up on Monday?"

"They do. And it's a roof leak in the men's dorm that lost you your hotel room. Sorry about that. They're on track with repairs though, so if you decide to switch to the hotel on Monday, they should be ready to have you."

"That's great. I don't want to kick you out of your home for longer than necessary." Mom had pushed—hard—for me to postpone the trip when I'd mentioned the housing situation. She didn't like putting someone out. Not that I relished it, but GG wanted me to come now. And Wendy had offered.

"It's no problem. My parents are glad for an excuse to have me back under their roof."

I laughed. "Doesn't seem to matter how old you get, does it?"

Wendy glanced over, and for the first time her smile seemed genuine. "No. No, it doesn't."

"We're blessed."

Her head cocked to the side slightly before she nodded. "I guess we are."

What did she mean by "I guess?" I didn't have the right to push. To question. But I wanted to. And that was unusual.

Before I could formulate a response, Wendy turned onto a tree-lined street. "This is the main entrance to the college. The building straight ahead is the chapel. The wings have classrooms in them."

I nodded and took in the brick building and its white bell tower. It wasn't imposing. It was welcoming.

"To the left is area we use for the passion play. We have an auditorium that seats two thousand, a large parking area, that sort of thing. In other seasons, we use it for graduation and there's a fall play as well, although it's not as widely attended. Still, our theater department has a solid reputation and several of our alumni have gone on to a career on the stage and screen." Wendy turned right.

"We're not going that way?"

She shook her head. "We'll do a circle and end there. Here's the administration building."

I listened as she told me about the history of each building and what was housed there. It was all information that I'd read in the packet she had emailed, but I didn't mind hearing her talk. She had a wisp of a drawl—one she'd clearly worked to eradicate—and there was a hint of something in her voice that drew me in and left me wondering about her.

Close to an hour later, she pulled into the driveway of a blue, two-story house. A porch wrapped around the ground level and a pair of rocking chairs sat to the left of the front door.

"Here we are." Wendy turned off the car and pushed open her door.

I hopped out of the car and hurried to the back, but she'd already opened the trunk and lifted down my suitcase and laptop bag. "I can get them."

"It's no problem. Come on in."

I frowned as she made her way up the path to the front door pulling my suitcase, my laptop bag over her shoulder. That was not how I was raised. But I also wasn't raised to tackle a woman and wrench my things out of her grasp. It was a conundrum, for sure.

I followed. The sun was setting, casting an impressive splash of colors across the sky behind the house. Wendy stood on the porch beside the open door.

I stepped through. "Thanks."

"Sure. The bedrooms are upstairs. You can choose whichever you want. All the sheets are fresh." Wendy grabbed my suitcase with both hands and began to hoist it up the stairs.

"Can you please let me get that?" I reached out and covered her hands with mine. "I can hear every woman in my family yelling at me in my head. It's really unpleasant."

Wendy laughed, but she set down the suitcase. "All right. I don't want to create an unpleasant headspace."

I let her keep the laptop bag. It wasn't worth the argument. Plus, she was already halfway up the stairs. I lifted the suitcase and followed.

At the top of the stairs, Wendy stopped and waited. When I joined her, she pointed down the hall. "The primary's down here. It has an en suite bathroom and a queen. The guest room is at the other end of the hall. It's just a double, but it's cozy. It shares the hall bath with the other two rooms. They're twin beds."

Her face had tightened with pain when she pointed to the

two doors that housed twin beds. It wasn't just a lack of desire to sleep in a single that kept me from choosing those.

"I'll take the guest room. A double is plenty, and I don't like the thought of evicting you from your room. Even if you're not staying there." I wanted to ask about a husband. She didn't wear a ring, but not everyone did. And it seemed odd to have such a large house if there was no family to share it with her.

Wendy didn't react. She just started down the hall toward the room. She set my laptop bag on the bed and glanced around, as if checking that everything was in order. "There's a set of keys on the island in the kitchen. I'll let you get settled and come back at around six to take you to dinner, if that works?"

"Sure. Thanks." I rolled my bag over to the closet and left it in front of the door. "I really appreciate you opening your home like this."

"It's no problem." Her expression didn't match her words.

"I don't mind figuring out dinner on my own, if you have things you need to do. If there's bread and peanut butter, I'll be happy."

"I can't do that to you your first night in town." Wendy slipped back through the door and started toward the stairs. "I'll be back at six."

"All right." I tucked my hands in my pockets and followed her. "Thanks again."

"Sure. Make yourself at home." Wendy glanced over her shoulder, smiled, and nodded once, then disappeared through the front door.

I blew out a breath and sank down on the top step. I had an hour to kill before dinner with the most enigmatic woman I'd met in my lifetime.

Time to unpack.

And maybe take a little look around.

5

WENDY

I woke up, groggy, and looked around. Dread settled in my stomach as I remembered where I was. And today was Saturday. No convenient excuse of hurrying to work like yesterday.

Oh, sure. I still had Mr. Swift—Preston—to deal with all day. But he'd said he planned to sleep in and then go for a run, so we'd made plans for me to head that way closer to lunchtime.

It was only six thirty a.m.

Dad was probably up. He'd been up before six every day of my life unless he was ill. There'd be fresh coffee. Maybe a Danish, if he'd run out to the bakery like he sometimes did on Saturday mornings.

I threw my legs over the side of the bed and forced myself to stand. Coffee and a pastry were enough reason to get up and face the day. If I was lucky, I'd get some caffeine and sugar into me before Mom started in with her questions and prodding.

Yes. Preston Swift was about my age.

Yes. He appeared to be single.

Yes. He was very nice looking.

But he didn't give off the impression that he'd come to

Gilead to do anything more than see the college. And set up that donation. I couldn't forget that.

I slid my feet into fuzzy slippers and snagged the zip-up hoodie off the top of my suitcase. I worked my arms into the sleeves as I shuffled across the room and opened the door to the hall. I paused, listening.

Nothing but the quiet creaks and pops of an old house greeted my ears.

That was good.

If Mom was up, she'd be talking already. She'd always been one to greet the morning with an outpouring of words. Dad and I had never understood it. Whitney had managed to roll with it a little better, although I don't think she would ever call herself a morning person either.

I tiptoed downstairs and into the kitchen. The digital display on the coffee pot said the brew had finished thirty minutes ago, and the smell of Dad's rich, Guatemalan dark roast filled the air. I didn't see Dad. Maybe he was in his workshop?

With a mental shrug, I opened the cabinet where Mom had kept mugs my whole life, and chose an oversized one. I didn't pay a lot of attention to what it said. My sister, Whitney, always said a funny saying made the coffee taste better, but I'd never noticed a difference. Then again, I was just in it for the caffeine. Sometimes, especially in the summer, I was just as happy to start my day with a cold can of pop.

I filled the mug, then dumped in two big spoons of sugar before heading to the fridge. Mom was a fan of flavored creamers. She had several varieties in the door. Gingerbread? Hmm. I pulled it out, flipped open the top, and sniffed. Why not?

I poured a generous slosh into my mug before replacing the creamer in the fridge. I stirred as I carried the mug over to the kitchen table and sat. I cradled the mug in my hands, breathing in the smell of coffee and sugar for several moments before sipping.

Mark would have hated it.

I pushed the thought away. Mark was gone. It shouldn't matter anymore what he thought of my need for large amounts of sugar in my coffee.

"There you are."

I glanced over as Dad wiped his feet on the mat just inside the kitchen door. "Morning, Daddy."

His grin flashed. "I wondered if you'd started sleeping in."

"Everyone sleeps in compared to you." I sipped my coffee. Dad and I had some variation of the same conversation any time we were in the same house in the morning. The reality though was that I would love to be able to sleep in like I used to. I'd give anything for a night full of slumber that wasn't ripped into three-hour shreds by nightmares and memories. "I was hoping you'd gone to the bakery."

"Thought about it. Decided risking your mother's wrath wasn't worth it. I'll scramble you some eggs if you want."

"Wrath? Why would Mom care about a Saturday bakery run?"

Dad shook his head. "She's convinced she gained ten pounds and has decided the two of us need to go on a diet together."

"But you didn't gain any weight." For that matter, I didn't think Mom had either. She certainly didn't look any different to me.

"Since when does that matter in a marriage?" Dad pulled open the fridge and got out the eggs. "I don't mind being supportive, since she hasn't banned bacon."

"I like bacon." I didn't eat a lot of it. Mom might have banned bakery items, but Mark had bordered on hating pork breakfast products. Even with him gone, I hadn't been brave enough to bring them back into the house.

"Thatta girl. I'll get it going in the oven and then fix us some eggs."

I sipped my coffee and watched as Dad returned to the fridge for a package of bacon. He turned on the oven and pulled out a baking sheet. Guilt pinged. "Can I help?"

He waved me off. "Nope. This is a one-man operation."

"Okay. Let me know if you change your mind."

"Tell me about your billionaire." Dad shot a wicked grin over his shoulder. "Does it really start with a 'b?'"

"For the family it does. I'm not sure of his personal net worth —I didn't dig much past the family money, since he said it was something his great-grandmother wanted done. I imagine there's a trust and he can access what he needs to set up an endowment. The Swifts have a big corner of the food industry, and have since the 1800s." Preston was the CEO of their family company. It was likely that his personal fortune started with a "b"—if not, the millions were certainly multiple. "He flew himself down. In his own plane. I talked to Gerald over at the airport, he said it's a six-person Cessna."

Dad slid the pan of bacon into the oven and moved to the sink to wash his hands. "He has his pilot license?"

"Apparently."

"Huh. That's a lot of time and effort."

And expense. I'd been curious enough to look it up. Not that money was a problem for him, but still.

"You're thinking something snarky." Dad pointed a finger at me before refilling his coffee and joining me at the table. "Spill it."

"It's not snarky. Really. Just a thought that piloting is a good sport for a rich guy."

Dad shook his head, his eyes sparkling with humor. "Or someone who enjoys flying. Maybe he thought he'd be a pilot instead of taking over the family fortune. Or he was going to join the Air Force and serve the country. There are all kinds of reasons someone might decide to learn to fly."

"Okay, okay. Sorry. Didn't mean to unfairly judge the rich guy."

"Mark's family is rich. Maybe not billionaire rich, but it isn't as if you didn't benefit from that." Dad watched me over the rim of his mug as he sipped.

I looked away. "No. You're right."

Dad sighed. "Have you heard from his parents at all?"

"No. I don't expect to, either. They made it clear that with Mark and the girls gone, I was nothing to them." It didn't hurt as much as it had at first. I'd known Mark's parents didn't love that we were together. But I'd thought they'd accepted me. Maybe even loved me in their own way. They certainly seemed to enjoy the girls. Well, when the girls behaved. Mark's parents hadn't had much use for children acting like children.

"That's their loss." Dad put down his coffee and touched my arm. "I'm sorry, honey."

I shrugged and took another, longer, drink. "It's fine."

He sent me a long look that made it clear he wasn't buying it. But what I loved about my dad was that he wouldn't push the issue. Mom would have. And if I hadn't given in and told her enough to make her feel like she got all the details, she would have called my therapist and suggested it as a topic of conversation.

How many times had my therapy appointment started with her letting me know the problem Mom thought I was having? Too many to count.

"Anyway. How long does that bacon take?" I glanced over at the oven.

"About twenty minutes. Are you telling me the only thing you know about the guy is that he's a pilot? You spent all day together yesterday."

I hunched my shoulders. I had spent the day with Preston yesterday. But that didn't mean I now knew everything there was to know about the guy. "I didn't give him the third degree. It's not like he's here to be quizzed about his life."

"So, what, you walked around in silence the whole day?"

"No, Dad." I set my mug down. "We talked about the school. I showed him the yearbooks that his great-grandparents were in. We spent a little more time in the archives digging around for other mentions, but the two of them were good at avoiding the college newspaper, so that was kind of a waste."

"Does he have a family?"

"I assume so. He mentioned brothers. He has a view of Lake Michigan from his house."

"Fancy."

I grinned. "Right? I did look that up online. It's right in line with that billions thing."

"What does he think of Kansas?"

"It's flat and there's wind." I laughed. "Same thing anyone new to the state mentions."

Dad nodded.

I studied him a moment. "You're not siding with Mom on this wacky idea that this is going to turn into something romantic, right?"

"Me? No. I don't meddle in my daughters' love lives."

That was mostly true. He didn't meddle as overtly as Mom, at least. But he wasn't above nudging here and there. Or encouraging Mom to meddle. "Good. Keep it that way."

"Still. I feel like you could do worse than a billionaire."

"Right. Because money is the only real qualification for a husband. Got it."

"I didn't say that. But it's obvious he's a believer, and—"

"Back up. How is that obvious? It's obvious his great-grandparents were believers enough that they were willing to sign the statement of faith to attend. That's it though."

Although, he had prayed before every meal that we'd shared and it hadn't seemed forced or as if he was doing it because it was expected.

"Okay. That's fair. So maybe that's what you ought to talk about with him today." Dad nodded as if it settled everything. "Then, once he passes that qualification, you can look at any others that might be on your list."

"I don't have a list, Dad. I'm content. I had Mark and the girls. I don't need to try to replace them."

"No one wants you to replace them, honey." Dad laid his hand on my arm. He left it there, the comforting warmth seeping through my sweatshirt. "But you know it's not good for man to be alone. God said that."

I nodded.

Mom kept hounding me about that, too. It might not be good for man to be alone, but I was feeling pretty good about the prospect as a woman.

6

PRESTON

I pulled open the door as soon as I saw Wendy's SUV turn into the driveway. I stepped out onto the porch and tugged the door closed, checking that the latch caught, then jogged down the steps and opened the car door.

Wendy looked over, eyebrows raised. "Sorry. Were you bored? There's a TV…"

"No. It's been a nice morning. I'm just excited to see the bell tower. That's our main adventure today, right?"

"That's the plan. I have the key to the stairwell and a flashlight, just in case the lights don't work."

I laughed. "Is that likely?"

She shrugged. "I'm not sure. I couldn't get a straight answer about the last time someone went up there."

"I thought it was a tradition that engaged couples went up and signed their names on the walls, then rang the bell." I frowned. GG had told me about it. Wendy hadn't acted surprised when I mentioned it.

"It did used to be the tradition. I don't think most people still bother though. Maybe if they're a legacy student."

"Define legacy student."

She glanced over. "Sorry. Academia term. Legacy students are people who are third and fourth generation coming to the school. It reaches a point where they have almost guaranteed admission and some of the family names carry weight."

"Interesting. Old money?"

"Not always. Just loyal to the school. Although, the majority of the legacy families do contribute. So it's not completely honest to say they aren't donors. But they're not all big money."

I nodded. "So the bell tower tradition isn't something you tell incoming freshmen?"

"Not to my knowledge. I only heard about it after graduating. I probably would have pushed to do it when my husband and I got engaged if I'd known about it. It sounds like one of those fun things you tell your grandchildren about, you know?"

I laughed. "I know exactly, since that's how GG views it."

I wanted to ask about her husband now that she'd brought him up, but I wasn't sure how to go about it. I cleared my throat. "I appreciate your husband being willing to give up his home for me."

"Oh." She looked over, her expression guarded. "He passed away."

"I'm sorry." I could have kicked myself. Super smooth.

"It's fine. You didn't know, and it's natural to be curious. It's been a little over a year. I'm doing fine."

I pressed my lips together to keep from saying something smart-aleky. Because it didn't sound like she was fine. Was she even expected to be fine after just a year? That felt fast. I tried to imagine losing someone I loved enough to have married. It was a stretch. I'd never loved someone like that. I dated. A little. Not enough to keep Mom happy, but enough to get her off my case.

"It was a car accident. I was in a coma. His parents had the funeral before I woke up. For him and our girls." She shrugged and then pulled into a parking spot in front of the chapel. "And now you know what everyone in town knows, although I'm sure if you ask around, you'll get some theories and juicy pieces of made-up information. My favorite is that the girls weren't really Mark's and I planned the accident to keep him from finding out."

My jaw dropped. I looked over at her, finally piecing together her behavior when she showed me through her house. She'd had kids and lost them tragically. My heart ached for her. Why would anyone in town make up horrible things in the face of such loss? "That makes no sense."

She gave a wan smile. "Small-town gossips don't put a lot of stock in sense. Not if it makes their story juicier. Come on. We've got stairs to climb."

I exited the car, still trying to wrap my head around the idea that someone would make up a story like that and spread it around. What possible reason was there for it? Especially when it was obvious Wendy was grieving.

"It's a nice, clear day. You'll get a great view from up there." Wendy pulled open the door to the chapel and gestured to the right. "The tower stairs are over here."

We crossed the chapel foyer. It had apparently been redecorated sometime in the nineties. The carpet was the same mottled gray I was used to seeing in church foyers. The oak trim gleamed from recent polishing. "Can I peek in?"

"Oh. Sure. Go ahead."

I went to a set of doors that led to the chapel proper and pulled one open. I'd been expecting pews, but there were auditorium-style seats filling the floor space. A large, raised stage lined the front of the room. Pipes filled the space behind the podium. "You have a pipe organ?"

"Yep. One of the first major purchases of the college. The music students still use it for recitals. And sometimes for the hymns during weekly chapels. It's lovely. I can ask and let you know when it's going to be used next, if you want to hear it."

"I might like that. Thanks."

She smiled. "Sure. Ready?"

"Yeah." I shot another look at the chapel. Had it been like that when GG was here? I pulled out my cellphone and snapped a picture. I'd ask her. Maybe she'd have a story about the organ. She'd always loved organ music. Had that enjoyment developed here?

"Here we are." Wendy put a key into the handle of an unobtrusive door bearing a simple brass plaque that stated "TOWER." She jigged the handle as she turned the key and it finally opened. She reached into the darkness beyond the door and, after a moment, there was a click. A tiny glimmer of light flickered on. "Well. It's better than nothing. Sort of."

"Guess it's good you brought the flashlight. After you."

"Oh, no. You're the guest."

I held her gaze a moment, then shrugged. I could probably make it up the stairs in dim light without making a complete fool of myself. I started up the tightly curling staircase, one hand resting lightly on the cold metal banister.

The door closed behind us with a solid *thunk*.

The light turned off.

I laughed. "I have brothers. This isn't scary."

"It wasn't me. Hang on, I'll pass you the flashlight."

I waited. It felt like a full minute before a circle of yellow light appeared on the stairs. Her feet shuffled on the steps, then her hand touched my arm.

I shifted and reached for the flashlight. "You really didn't turn the light off?"

"I really didn't. And believe me, I'm going to mention that the door closing shut off the light. That doesn't seem like it's safe."

I nodded and started back up the stairs. "It could be the bulb. If it's old, and it got shaken, it could have broken the filament."

"You do a lot with lightbulbs, do you?"

I heard the snark in her voice and ignored it. So what. Maybe it was common knowledge, but didn't most people use LED bulbs these days? They didn't have the problem incandescent bulbs did. And okay, fine, my grandfather had played around with making his own lightbulbs for a while when I was a teen. I thought the glass blowing was cool, so I'd stuck around and tried to help. Turned out there wasn't a market for custom lightbulbs. Grandmother had said as much when he'd floated the idea, but she'd also indulged him. It wasn't as if they needed him to be out earning an income.

"I know a lot of useless things."

"Oh yeah? Tell me something useless."

I searched through the trivia in my brain. "Did you know helium was discovered at the University of Kansas?"

She chuckled. "I did not. And you're right, that's pretty useless. Why do you know that?"

I shrugged. I wasn't sure if she could see it or not, but I also didn't really care. "I like learning things."

We climbed the rest of the stairs in silence, the only sound our feet on the steps. I was struggling to keep my breathing even as we neared the top. Wendy was puffing like a steam train.

Finally, we reached another door.

I tried the handle. "This one's locked, too."

Wendy held up a finger and sucked in a deep breath. She let it out. "Obviously I need to do more stair climbing."

I grinned.

She dug the keys out of her pocket and fitted one into the doorknob. This handle turned more easily than the one below had. When she pushed the door open, a wave of mustiness rolled out.

I coughed. Clearly, no one had been up here in a while. I shone the light in the room and grinned. Names covered every inch of the walls. Big printing. Smaller script. Some had hearts drawn around them. One couple had made a pencil sketch of their faces—or at least I assumed it was them—beside their names.

"This is incredible." I stepped into the room and played the light over the walls.

Wendy flipped a light switch and a bulb flickered to life. She moved to one of the walls and ran her fingers under a set of names.

I looked over, but couldn't immediately associate the name with her. Maybe she was just excited about the history of it.

GG had told me, generally, where she thought their names would be. She wouldn't admit it, and none of us would ever push it, at her age, but her memory wasn't always as sharp as she'd like. I looked around, trying to get my bearings against the description GG had given, and inched my way toward the far side of the room. Over near the corner, I squatted.

There it was. "Edna and George" in GG's unmistakable cursive surrounded by a heart.

"Did you find it?"

I glanced up. Wendy had moved closer.

"I did." I shone the light on it.

Wendy's sigh was wistful. "They had a happy marriage?"

"They did. At least from everything I ever observed and things my mom said. Not that they didn't disagree. Great-grandpa could be formidable when he got riled. But GG could always hold her own and help him calm down." I set the flashlight down. I didn't really need it now that the overhead light had warmed up. I got my phone out of my pocket and took a few photos. "Thanks for bringing me up here."

"Sure. I'm glad you asked about it. It's the kind of thing I know, but never really think about. If that makes any sense."

I stood from my squat, my knees protesting. "It does. Was the name over there from your family?"

"What? Oh." She chuckled and shook her head. "No. It's a missionary couple. One of many that our school has trained and helped send out. They were killed in Papua New Guinea three or four years after they graduated."

I blinked. I probably should have some kind of response to that, but my mind had gone blank.

"Anyway. Do you want to ring the bell while you're up here?" Wendy gestured to the rope that dangled from above and disappeared through a hole in the floor. To make it easier for people to ring the bell without having to climb all those stairs? Probably. I didn't remember seeing the rope down on the ground floor. But I also hadn't been looking.

"No. I think I'm good."

She laughed. "All right. Then I guess it's time to head back down."

"Down has to be easier than up. Right?" I grinned at her obvious reluctance to start the descent.

"Maybe. It's still more stairs than I usually do."

"Me, too." I started toward the door. "But we can't stay here forever."

"Yeah, yeah." Wendy's hand flew up to cover her mouth. "I'm so sorry."

I laughed. It was nice to see a crack in her extremely professional demeanor. "Wow. Just like that, you lose a million."

She paled and her eyes widened.

I held up my hands and tried not to laugh even harder. "Kidding. I promise."

"It's all fun and games until I have a heart attack and you have to lug my dead body down all those stairs." Wendy brushed past me into the hall, pausing to flip off the light.

For a fleeting moment, I imagined what it would be like to pick her up and toss her over my shoulder. Of course, in my bizarre little fantasy, she was laughing and pretending to protest while she hammered at my back with her fists. Then I'd put her down and back her up against a wall and...oh man. What was I doing?

Realizing she'd continued to speak, I cleared my throat. "Sorry. Missed that."

"I asked if you minded pulling the door shut. Are you okay?" She was looking at me like I'd grown another head.

My face burned. I turned for the door, checked that the lock was twisted, and tugged it closed. "Yeah. I'm good. Just got lost in thought for a minute."

Wendy nodded once. "I do that, sometimes."

Probably not the same way I just had, but I'd leave that alone. Wendy was a lovely woman. I couldn't—wouldn't—deny it. But that didn't mean I needed to have caveman fantasies about her. She was a widow. And according to her, it was more than a year ago and she was fine, so maybe she already had someone new. The fact that she'd given up her house suggested she was unattached—but it wasn't a guarantee.

We started down the stairs, our footsteps echoing as we descended.

I cleared my throat again. "So. What are your plans for the rest of your Saturday?"

"No plans. I'm completely at your disposal."

I frowned. "But it's Saturday. You're not working today, are you?"

She shrugged.

Maybe I imagined it, but I thought I saw her hand contract

on the stair rail. "Donor relations isn't always a weekday thing. It's fine. I'm used to it. And it gets me out of the house, which I appreciate."

"I mean, I kind of already kicked you out of your house."

She glanced over and managed a hint of a smile. "So you did. Getting out of Mom and Dad's is a good thing, too."

I nodded. "I can see that. Parents mean well."

"They do." She stepped down off the final stair and reached for the doorknob. "They just don't always know what to do about it."

I tipped my head to the side and looked at her. Maybe for the first time, I did more than notice how attractive she was. She had circles under her eyes. Oh, they were covered with makeup, but they couldn't hide from deeper study. Her eyes themselves were tired. And sad.

"That sounds like a story."

She shook her head. "You couldn't possibly be interested."

"But I am."

Her lips thinned as she pressed them together and her index finger drummed on her leg. After a moment, she lifted one shoulder. "How do you feel about pasta?"

"I like pasta."

"If you really want to hear the story, I'll come over, make you dinner, and give you the scoop. I'd just as soon it came from me. Everyone in town knows the details anyway. Of course, they all have their own little spin they like to add. You're missing out on some creative fiction."

I snickered. "I always prefer truth to fiction."

"All right." She twisted her arm to look at her watch. "I'll drop you off at the house and then I need to run and get some things from the store."

"I've been known to visit the grocery store. I can just tag along."

Little lines formed on her forehead when she frowned. She clearly wanted to tell me no. But politeness—and probably her knowledge of my family's financial status—warred with her instinct. She sighed. "Fine. I don't think you know what you're getting into though."

"It's a grocery store. What's there to get into?"

She snorted.

My eyebrows lifted at the unladylike sound. I watched her pull the door closed and check that it was secured. I didn't understand her concern. I bought groceries all the time at home. Nobody batted an eye. Sure, my family had money, but it wasn't as if my face was recognizable to people on the street.

7

WENDY

The drive to the grocery store didn't take long, which was a blessing. Preston had gone quiet and spent the time looking out the window. I tried to imagine what he thought when he saw the town. Brick buildings. Brick main street. And the eerie flatness of Kansas fields stretching out beyond them.

Maybe he saw something more poetic. Maybe he was trying to picture his great-grandparents here. It wouldn't take much imagination. The town hadn't changed a lot over the years.

I wished, again, that Preston had taken me up on the offer to drop him back at my house instead of tagging along. Maybe in Chicago the grocery store was just a place to buy food. But here? In Gilead, Kansas? Showing up at the grocery store with an attractive man in tow was guaranteed to fuel the old lady gossip circuit for at least a month. Especially if Mrs. Alleghany was there. Since the woman seemed to visit the grocery store every day for one thing or another, the probability was incredibly high that she was.

I glanced over at Preston and fought back a sigh. It really was too bad he wasn't old and ugly.

Or young and ugly.

The "ugly" was the important part, and even then, as a wealthy man, Mrs. Alleghany would probably have plenty to say about how looks weren't that important in the overall scheme of things. But Mark had been handsome, and she'd made enough comments to me in the last six months—six months of mourning apparently being her upper limit for acceptable—about how I needed to find another good-looking man.

I signaled and turned into the parking lot in front of the grocery store and headed for a spot in the second row. All the close ones were taken.

"You can wait in the car, if you want." Was it too much to hope he'd take me up on it?

Preston's eyebrows lifted almost to his hairline. "I don't mind coming in. Maybe I'll grab a bag of cookies or something for late night munching."

"Sure." I managed a tight smile before I reached for my purse and opened the car door. I sent up a quick prayer that we could get in and out without a big fuss. I didn't actually believe God was listening though. He and I did a lot of talking past one another, it seemed. Or willful misunderstanding.

I dragged my thoughts away from that and started toward the front door without even checking to see if Preston was coming.

The doors slid open as we approached. I snagged one of the smaller carts and dropped my purse in the top.

"Want me to push?" Preston laid his hand on the cart handle.

"I've got it. I don't need much." I pointed the cart toward the produce section and paused. "Cookies are in aisle six if you want to peruse. I can meet you there."

"I don't mind tagging along."

"K." I struggled to get the frustration out of my voice. "Pesto or alfredo?"

"Uh. I like them both."

I nodded. Of course he did. I'd just check and see if Bed of Greens, a local truck farm, had been able to refresh their herb supply. There'd been an issue with the greenhouses in the fall. It was the talk of the town that they'd had to lay off a lot of workers this year. I didn't care about that so much, but I wasn't excited about the replacements they'd had to arrange at the grocery store.

If there was good basil, we'd go pesto. If not, alfredo.

I paused in front of the herbs. There was some basil. Enough for pesto? Maybe if I cleaned out the section. I hated to do that, though. I grabbed one bunch and set it in the cart. "Looks like we'll be having alfredo. Maybe that's better, anyway. It's chilly outside."

"I'm not following. But I like alfredo."

"Warm sauce versus cold?" At least Preston, unlike Mark, would say something when he didn't understand my train of thought. And I did *not* need to be comparing Preston to Mark. I didn't even need to be thinking of Mark.

Crash!

The impact of my cart smashing into another jolted up my arms. "I'm sorry. I'm so sorry. I wasn't paying attention."

The man I'd hit waved away my words. "It's good."

I tipped my head to the side and looked at him. He was familiar. But also not someone I immediately recognized. I didn't have a chance to say anything before Preston spoke.

"Dawson? You're Dawson, right?" Preston moved around the cart; his hand outstretched. "What are you doing in Kansas?"

The man—who was apparently Dawson—laughed and shook Preston's hand. "I could ask you the same thing."

Preston glanced back at me. "My great-grandmother graduated from the Bible college. I'm here to work on setting up an endowment."

"Nice. I'm the new head of their AV department." Dawson gave a little shrug. "Or I will be when I start on Monday."

That was it. That was why I recognized him. HR had sent out an email with a photo and bio mentioning that he'd be starting in January.

"Excellent. Congrats. Although, I guess that means we won't bump into each other in Chicago."

"Who knows? I might get roped into coming back for some stuff. And apparently, we're bumping into each other in Kansas now." Dawson grinned.

Preston chuckled. "So we are. Good to see you."

"You, too." Dawson maneuvered his cart away from mine and strolled away.

"Small world." Preston shook his head.

"I guess so." I started toward the cheese section. "Friends in Chicago, were you?"

"Who? Dawson and me? Nah. We just bump into each other enough at some of the big fundraising events that we're nodding acquaintances."

My definition of nodding acquaintance was obviously different than Preston's, but I let it slide. I considered the blocks of Parmesan and grabbed one that looked like it would be enough for the sauce and still leave some for grating on top. I started along the back wall of the store. "Now I just need eggs and we'll be ready."

"You put eggs in your pasta in Kansas?" Preston fell into step beside me.

"Flour, eggs, sometimes water if it's too dry. I'm pretty sure that's how they make pasta everywhere." I stopped in front of the case with cartons of eggs and forced a smile. "Hello, Mrs. Alleghany."

The woman glanced up from the open carton of eggs in her

hand, and her eagle eyes zeroed in on Preston a moment before moving back to me. "Wendy, dear, how are you?"

"I'm doing well. Thanks. Yourself?"

"Oh, I can't complain."

I barely managed to hold back a snort of derision. Mrs. Alleghany loved two things in life—gossip and complaining about her ailments. But no one was ever going to call her on either. "That's good. It's always better to focus on gratitude, right?"

"Always." Her gaze flicked over to Preston. "I don't believe I recognize your young man."

I didn't bother with a denial. She'd just say it was protesting too much or something else that bordered on asinine. "May I present Preston Swift? He's in town from Chicago. His great-grandparents are alumni. Preston, this is Mrs. Alleghany. She's a fixture in town."

"Pleasure to meet you." Preston extended his hand.

I reached for a carton of eighteen eggs and flipped open the lid to check that none were broken.

"The pleasure's mine. How long are you in town?"

"Oh, I'm not sure yet. Maybe a week?" Preston tucked his hands in his pockets. "I just wanted to get a feel for things."

"Hmm." Mrs. Alleghany's eyes sparkled.

I closed my eyes for a moment, dreading just how she was going to spread that little nugget around. A feel for things. Ugh.

"There's not much in your cart, dear. Are you going out to eat?"

"No, ma'am. I'm making pasta and an alfredo sauce. I have everything else I need for that at home."

She nodded once before turning her attention back to Preston. "And where are you staying while you're in town? I heard the hotels were housing students through tomorrow at least."

"Wendy was gracious enough to let me stay at her home."

I jumped in before she could respond to that seemingly sala-cious tidbit. "I've been at my parents' house since he arrived."

"Ah." She eyed me a moment before nodding and reaching over to pat my cheek. "You've always been a good girl."

"We should get going. It was lovely to see you." I started to push the cart toward the exit.

"Tell your parents hello from me."

"I will." I lifted my hand and hurried my steps without looking back. That had been about as terrible as I'd imagined it was going to be. I pushed my basket to the open lane and unloaded the items onto the conveyor.

"Should I apologize?" Preston eyed the candy on the rack and grabbed two Snickers. He set them behind the eggs.

"No. You're fine. She was going to find a way to make it sensa-tional no matter what we did." It was what Mrs. Alleghany did. I knew it, but it didn't make it any easier to swallow. Everyone in town just put up with her gossipy nature. Some even tried to make it sound like the woman was quaint and a charming, necessary part of any small town worth its salt. But I would happily go the rest of my life without being at the mercy of her smug smirks and pretend sympathy.

The cashier scanned the items quickly and I handed over cash to cover the cost before Preston could dig his wallet out of his pocket.

"I can—"

"No." I shook my head and met his gaze. "Seriously. I've got it."

The cashier's eyebrows lifted and I fought a sigh, sure that little interaction would make the rounds as well.

"Have a great day."

"Yeah. You, too." I lifted my hand in a brief wave and grabbed the bag of groceries.

"I can at least carry the bag." Preston's warm hand brushed mine as he reached for the plastic loops.

I fought off the sensation of his touch—I was definitely not going to analyze that—and let him take the bag. "You just want your candy."

"True words." He grinned and reached into the bag to grab one of the chocolate bars.

"Don't spoil your supper." The words were automatic. I'd spent too many years as a mom to keep them from slipping out. My throat tightened.

"No worries on that front. My mom insists that someday my metabolism will slow down and I'll end up gaining weight, but it hasn't happened yet. She insists it's unfair, since thirty-five was when she started to have to pay more attention to her weight." He shrugged and reached for the car door, then pulled it open for me before heading around to the passenger seat.

I blinked, then climbed behind the wheel.

"Anyway," Preston set the groceries at his feet, closed his car door, fastened his seatbelt, and then ripped open the candy. "Dad never had a problem, so I'm pretty sure I'll be fine."

I watched him bite off a solid quarter of the candy bar in one chomp. Shaking my head, I started the engine and pointed the car toward the house. "Are you really staying for a whole week?"

"Should I not?" He bit off another enormous chunk of chocolate, caramel, and peanuts.

At least he didn't smack his lips together when he chewed. Mark had been a lip smacker. I shuddered.

"If you're cold, you can bump the heat up. This isn't all that different from Chicago, but I'm fine either way." Preston reached for the dial on the dashboard and adjusted the temperature himself.

"Thanks." It was easier than trying to explain. "You're welcome to stay as long as you want. I just don't know what else to show you at the college. Unless you want to audition for the passion play?"

Preston snorted.

I glanced over. "What? You could. Auditions are open and the play is kind of a big deal. In fact, it's pretty much our big claim to fame. I'm sure your great-grandmother mentioned it."

"I guess she said something about it. Still, no thanks. Acting isn't my thing."

"Okay." I certainly wasn't going to push. My parents had always insisted on us being part of the play in one way or another growing up. I'd been in the ensemble more times than I cared to count. Now that I worked for the college, I tried to find ways to stay in the background as much as possible. "Well, auditions start Monday. I usually try to observe when I can, and you're more than welcome to join me. Maybe you'll change your mind."

"I just don't see that happening, but I appreciate the offer."

I nodded and turned the car into the driveway. It was good to be home. Even if I wasn't going to be able to stay, not being at my parents' house was still a bonus. I cut the engine and pushed open the door.

Preston was already getting out of his side, the bag of groceries in his hand. I watched him for a moment. If I was someone else—someone who wasn't irreparably broken—I might be tempted to flirt with him. See if there was anything that could develop there. He was handsome. At least, I thought so. And rich.

That had to count, right?

Even in my head, it sounded snarky. I knew that "rich" meant diddly when it came to the kind of person someone was. Mark had come from money. Maybe not billions, like Preston, but his family had rubbed elbows with all the people who mattered. And a small-town girl from Kansas was definitely not who they'd envisioned for their son.

"Stop it." I hissed the words under my breath.

Preston turned, one foot on the bottom step of the porch. "Sorry?"

"Nothing. Talking to myself." My cheeks were burning. I could picture just how bright red they must be. And there was nothing to do about it. Not one thing.

"I do that a lot." He winked and gestured for me to go ahead of him onto the porch.

I blamed the stutter of my heart on the embarrassment. It couldn't be anything else. "I'm sorry to hear that. They say it's not exactly a sign of a healthy mental state."

He laughed and followed me through the front door and into the kitchen. "Only if you're having drawn-out conversations."

"Ah. Okay then." I wasn't going to admit that was exactly what I did. It was better if he thought I was just someone who liked to hear my own voice now and then. I tapped the island as I walked to the sink to wash my hands. "Go ahead and set the groceries here. It'll take me about an hour to make dinner."

"Okay." Preston set the bag down, then looked at me expectantly. "How can I help?"

8

PRESTON

Wendy very obviously wanted me to go anywhere other than the kitchen and leave her alone while she cooked. If I was a better man, I'd probably do just that, but there was something about being around her.

Plus, she'd said she was going to make pasta. Like *make* the noodles. I had to see how that got done. I wasn't the world's worst cook, but I'd certainly never attempted to make noodles. Not when I could pick up a box of them at the grocery store for a couple of bucks and they'd just be there in the pantry when I got around to wanting them.

"You want to help?" The way her voice went up at the end of the sentence made me grin. She *really* didn't want me to stay.

"Yeah. Least I can do. You're making me pasta. From scratch."

Wendy blew out a breath and her bangs fluttered slightly. She studied me for a moment before nodding. "Get the flour out of the pantry for me. It's in a canister."

I'd seen her pantry. I'd stumbled across it by accident, thinking the door led to a powder room. Maybe that was how it had started its life. I crossed the kitchen and opened the pantry door. I still couldn't quite put into words the idea of a walk-in pantry. If Mom or Grandma got a glimpse of this, they'd be calling up architects and planning a remodel before I could blink. The bottom of the space was lined with cabinets and drawers. There was a counter that went all around three sides of the room. Open shelves reached from there to the ceiling. All the wood was painted a sunny yellow. Somehow, it avoided being blinding.

I scanned the canisters that sat on the counter and finally found the large one labeled "flour." I grabbed it and headed back out to the kitchen.

"Thanks." Wendy reached for it and pried off the top. She scooped flour onto the counter, and pushed it up into a hill, then she hollowed out the middle like it was the crater of a volcano. She picked up a bowl and tipped the contents—eggs, it appeared—into the divot.

My phone rang.

I fished it out of my pocket and my lips tipped up. "Excuse me."

Wendy made a shooing motion. "Go. It's fine."

I accepted the call and started walking out into the foyer. "Hi, GG."

"There you are, sweet boy. How's Gilead?"

GG was the only one who could get away with any of the nicknames I'd had as a kid. Sweet boy seemed to be her favorite. "It's small."

She chuckled. "City boy. Like your great-grandfather."

"Guilty. I definitely miss Chicago. Even that dreadful condo."

"Oh, poor baby, up there in a penthouse looking out at Lake Michigan."

I hunched my shoulders. No one could deliver a reprimand like GG. I cleared my throat. "Did you get the pictures I texted you?"

"I did." GG's sigh ended with a bit of a wheeze. "I remember writing our names like it was yesterday. I wish I could have come with you."

I sank onto the stairs and leaned my head against the wall. "That would have been fun. Want me to fly home and spring you?"

"I love that you'd ask."

She didn't say it, but I knew. The medical staff at her assisted living home was very clear that GG was in no shape to leave. They didn't expect her to live to see her birthday in June. Mom tap danced around it. My brothers all took their lead from her. It would be left to me to handle, like everything else. "Say the word, GG, and I'll figure out how to make it happen."

"Who was with you? She's lovely."

"When?"

"In the photos you sent. I couldn't get a completely clear look."

"Oh. That's Wendy Hall. She's the woman from the college who's in charge of development. She's been very helpful."

"And is that all?"

I shifted on the stair, suddenly noticing how firm it was. "I'm not sure what else there could be."

"Preston."

"GG." I shook my head. She was always looking for romantic entanglements. And okay, for just a moment when our hands had brushed, I'd felt...something. Probably static from the cold, dry air. "She's a very nice woman who's simply doing her job."

"Hm. Well, I'd still love to see a better photo of her. I'm sure if you let her know you're humoring your great-grandmother, she'll be fine with it. After all, you're donating a couple hundred million dollars."

I choked on the air I was in the process of breathing in. "Couple of hundred...GG. We never talked about that much."

"It's not as if we don't have it."

I drew in a deep breath. That depended on how you looked at it. "I'd planned to set something up that would be more of an annuity. I just don't think it's smart to donate a big lump sum."

"Well. You're the businessman. I'll defer to you, but I want it to be significant."

"It will be. Do you need your name on a building? Or great-granddad's? I'm sure they'll ask about that. I can make it a requirement."

"Oh, no. Nothing like that. I just want to know it's possible for future generations to go there and experience the play."

"The play?"

Whitney had mentioned that. GG never had before. Her college memories tended to circle around meeting and falling in love with great-granddad.

"Oh, yes. The passion play they do every year. You need to see it. It's so memorable. So moving. The crucifixion of Jesus acted out. You can't watch it and not realize the depth of horror our Savior went through because He loves us."

"I'll make a point of getting back down here to see it then."

"You aren't staying in Gilead?"

"GG, I have work in Chicago. A life." Such as it was. More work than life. And okay, I could probably do everything I needed to do remotely, but it seemed like an unnecessary step. And living in a hotel until...when? Easter? That didn't appeal at all.

"I'm sure you know best. I love you, Preston. Send me that picture. I have to go."

I looked at my phone when the call ended abruptly. What was going through her head? I didn't need to stay down here. I hadn't needed to come down here in the first place. I'd only agreed to handle this myself instead of letting the lawyers talk to the school because GG insisted.

And GG had insisted again that I come down.

But I thought for sure she only meant for me to stay a weekend. See the college. Go up to the bell tower and get that photo. Then come home to Chicago and let the lawyers figure the rest of it out.

Sighing, I stood and slipped my phone back into my pocket before heading toward the kitchen.

Wendy was cranking a handle on a silver machine that seemed to be clipped to the counter. Pale yellow dough went in the top and came out in a thin sheet at the bottom.

"That's the pasta?"

"It is. Everything all right at home?"

I nodded and pulled out a stool at the counter. "That was my GG. I sent her a picture of their names. She actually wanted a picture of you. Is that okay?"

Wendy's hand paused on the crank and her eyebrows lifted. "Why would she want a picture of me?"

I gave a little shrug. "I guess I got a little of you in one of the pictures of the bell tower. She likes to see the people I work with."

A line formed between her eyebrows as she looked at me. Finally, she resumed cranking. "I guess that's fine."

"Thanks." I got my phone back out and took a photo.

"Wait. Not now." She glanced down at herself then back at me. "I thought you would wait until I wasn't in the middle of cooking."

"You look nice."

She snorted and fed the dough into a different opening on the top of her machine. This time when she turned the crank, thin noodles came out the bottom. She dusted them with flour and then leaned over a pot to peer into it before adjusting a knob on the stove. The fire underneath grew.

"We're just about ready. I hope you're hungry."

"It smells delicious. What's that?" I pointed to the saucepan where something white simmered.

"Cream and butter. It's about ready for the Parmesan. You wanted to help, right?"

"Sure."

She handed me a long, thin grater and a block of cheese. "Perfect. Grate the cheese into the cream, then use the wooden spoon to stir it together."

I stood and moved around to her side of the cooktop. "How much?"

"I'll tell you when." She scooped the noodles off the counter and dropped them in the bigger pot, which I could now see was filled with boiling water.

I ran the cheese over the grater. Delicate strands of cheese floated into the cream and butter. "What's this called? The grater thing."

"Microplane. Why?"

"I might want one. It's cool."

Wendy laughed. "Pause and stir."

I did as she instructed. She nodded and pointed to the cheese again. I picked it up and grated more. She wasn't kidding about using all of it. I was having to watch my fingertips when she finally spoke again.

"That should be good. Stir it again."

I set the microplane aside and picked up the spoon. The sauce had thickened quite a bit. The rich, nutty smell of the cheese filled the air.

Wendy lifted part of the pot, and water drained through the tiny holes. She gave it a couple of good shakes then nudged me aside and dumped the noodles into the sauce. When she'd set the strainer back into the pot of water, she grasped the handle of the pan and gave the pasta and sauce a few expert flips like I'd seen TV chefs do. The one and only one time I'd tried doing something like that, I'd ended up flinging food all over the kitchen and making do with a bowl of cereal.

"Impressive."

She flashed a grin. "Thanks. We're ready, if you want to get plates for me?"

"Sure." I liked the way she assumed I knew where things were. I'd only been staying in her house a few days, so it wasn't necessarily a given. It wasn't as if I'd been here for many meals. She'd made it a point to take me out for lunch and dinner yesterday. Even so, I had been here for breakfast and I'd done my share of snooping.

Or exploring. Which was what I preferred to call it.

I opened the cupboard that held the plates and got down two, then set them on the counter near the stove before heading for the drawer that held the flatware to get forks.

"Do you want to eat in the dining room?" I'd had my breakfast at the counter, but maybe pasta with someone else meant we should at least try to be civilized?

"Oh. Sure. We can." Wendy picked up the two plates, now full of pasta, and started in that direction.

I caught up to her as she hesitated in the doorway. It seemed as though she took a deep breath before stepping in and moving toward the table.

"Where would you like to sit?"

Something about her voice had changed. I frowned slightly. "Anywhere is fine. Just don't put us at opposite ends. I don't need to shout to have a conversation."

She managed a wan smile and set one plate down on the side of the table before she carried the other around to the opposite seat. She set that plate down and sat. "How's this?"

I took my seat and slid a fork across the table to her. "Perfect. Can I bless the food?"

"Sure." Wendy folded her hands in her lap and bowed her head.

After a moment, I followed suit and offered a short prayer for the food, trying to keep my focus on the words that I said and not the sense of vague disappointment that she hadn't offered her hand before the blessing.

"Amen."

I looked up to see Wendy's tight smile before she picked up her fork and twirled it in the pasta.

I speared a noodle and wrapped it around my fork, tipping it to adhere more of the cheesy sauce before bringing it to my mouth. The salty and creamy sauce accented the slightly eggy flavor of the noodles. I closed my eyes. "Mmm."

"I'm glad you like it."

That seemed like an understatement. "I could eat this every day for the rest of my life. I'm not sure I've ever eaten fresh pasta before."

"I doubt that. There are plenty of fancy restaurants in Chicago who make their own. I'm positive of that."

I nodded. "Probably so. I try to avoid fancy whenever possible."

She laughed.

"I'm serious. Give me fresh fries from the golden arches any day versus a pretentious dining room where I have to wear a tie and it seems like the price of the plate goes up in direct proportion to how small the portions are." I took another bite of pasta.

"Well. I guess we should have hit the drive through instead."

I grinned at her and shook my head. "No way. This is way better. Plus, your dining room is cozy."

She looked around the room like she was trying to see it through my eyes. "If you say so."

"I do. You've got a great sense of style. The whole house is warm and welcoming without being stuffy. I should show you photos of my condo. Then you'll understand." I put my fork down and dug my phone out of my pocket. I scrolled to the website for the designer—because she had the place as a separate page for prospective clients—and slid it across the table.

Wendy took the phone. Her eyebrows lifted as she scrolled, but she didn't speak.

I went back to eating. Would she ask how I could stand it? I wouldn't know how to answer that, honestly. I just lived there. And did some work. But it was certainly a motivation for me to go into the office more often than not. Who wanted to work surrounded by ornate gilt everything? Not me.

She cleared her throat.

I looked up.

She pushed the phone back over to me. "It doesn't seem very...you."

I laughed. "Understatement."

Wendy tipped her head to the side.

I took it as an invitation to explain. "It's technically my grandma's place. Dad's mom. She's very into the family money and prestige and appearance. And that sounds like she's some kind of materialistic harridan, but she isn't. It's just...hard to explain. Anyway, she and Mom bought a house a few blocks away and as the oldest, Grandma decided I should live in the condo."

"Do you like it?"

"I like the views. And the outdoor space. And if I redecorated, I'd probably love it."

"So why don't you?"

"I guess mostly because it's not really my place. It's Grandma's. And she spent a lot getting it just so." I shrugged. I hadn't actually asked about changing things. "I don't really think of it as more than a place to live. It's not home, if you know what I mean?"

After a moment, Wendy nodded slowly.

"Anyway, GG thinks I should stay here and participate in the play." I wasn't sure why I'd said that out loud. It wasn't as if I was going to follow through on it.

"You should. Absolutely."

I stared at Wendy. "Really? I'm not...I don't know anything about acting."

"I'm sure we can find you something else to do. Your family business is food service. We have concessions."

I snapped my mouth shut and looked down at my nearly empty plate. I didn't want to stay here. I'd planned on brushing off GG's suggestion. And I'd expected Wendy to laugh politely and give a noncommittal answer of some sort. I certainly hadn't expected her to agree that I should stay.

So why had she?

And why did that fact make me want to consider it more seriously?

9

WENDY

After the day I'd had at work, the very last thing I wanted to do was sit in on another round of auditions. It was the third day of five, and I was ready for the process to be over. Except, of course, that there hadn't been enough people to fill all the roles yet.

I hadn't seen Preston since Saturday evening.

I'd invited him to church, but he'd declined. He'd decided to fly back to Chicago, instead. I couldn't blame him. If I had a quick and easy way to get out of Gilead and never look back? I'd be gone so fast, people would think there'd been a tornado.

Of course, I couldn't tell anyone that. Or ever let on that I felt that way.

My parents had dealt pretty well with my sister, Whitney, leaving as soon as she could. But they'd also spent the better part of the last ten years going on and on about how glad they were that I'd stayed and how nice it was to have someone around. They'd been thrilled when Mark had moved to remote work so we could stay in Gilead. When the girls had been born? They were even more elated.

Now?

I sighed.

Now I'd become their project. And I was tired of being someone's project.

I pushed the thoughts aside. I wasn't going to solve any of them by sitting in my office thinking about them, and if I spent too much more time hiding—because let's face it, that was what I was doing—I'd be sneaking into the auditions after they started. That would surely garner a glare, possibly a reprimand, from the casting directors.

"Let's go, Wendy." I'd hoped the audible encouragement would get me moving, but instead I just sat there. "Get over it."

"Get over what?"

I jolted and spun toward the office door. "Preston?"

He grinned. "You didn't get my voicemail."

I'd seen a voicemail notification on my cell, but when I tried to check it, there'd been some weird goof and I hadn't been able to figure out how to restore it after I accidentally deleted it. "Technical issues. No. Why didn't you call back?"

"Well, I told you that I only needed to hear back from you if there was a problem. So I figured no news was good news." Preston shrugged. "Obviously, I need to rethink my voicemail strategy."

I didn't know what to say to that. I cleared my throat. "How long are you in town?"

"Through Easter. GG is pretty insistent."

My eyebrows lifted. "Where will you stay?"

"I guess I'm going to be calling the hotel and hoping for tonight. Then looking around for an apartment."

There were a handful of apartment buildings, but it was unlikely that he'd find something empty. Not at the start of the semester. Some of the buildings had a two-year waitlist attached to them. Students couldn't wait to be allowed to live off campus. "Let me guess. You asked me to get you some leads on a place to stay."

He nodded.

I winced. "Sorry. I can pack a quick bag and you can stay at my place again. My parents would be thrilled to have me back."

"No. I can't do that to you again. I'm sure it'll be fine." He tipped his head to the side. "What were you getting over when I got here?"

My lips curved in spite of myself. "The need to go sit through auditions. Why don't you join me?"

"You know I'm not trying out for a part in the play, right?"

"Sure. But your great-grandmother wants you to get a feel for the whole experience. This is how it starts. Plus, we'd discussed —briefly—the idea of you helping with concessions. I'm pretty sure Letty will be there with snacks tonight, so you can meet her and see what she'll need you to do."

"I..." Preston trailed off. He seemed to be thinking it over a moment, then shrugged. "All right."

I stood. Suddenly, the prospect of spending the evening listening to people reading from a script didn't seem so bad. Not if Preston was going to be nearby.

I didn't analyze it. I would need to. But that could wait. "All right, let's go. How'd you get here from the airport?"

"I flew commercial this time. Landed in Wichita. Bought a car and drove over."

"*Bought* a car?" I stopped and looked at him.

"Cheaper in the long run than renting. I can drive it home when I go back. Or sell it." His shrug was casual. "And this way, you don't have to babysit me. I know that's not reasonable long term."

I nodded once, dazed. What must it be like to be able to just buy a car like it was no big deal? To not have to weigh the pros and cons of financing options or try to milk a few more miles out of the current junker and save up? "Well. Do you remember the way to the auditorium?"

"Sure. Plus the campus is well marked. I'll meet you there?"

"Sounds good." I double-checked that I had everything I needed, flipped off the light, and pulled my office door closed behind me. We made small talk on the short walk from my office to the parking lot and I gave a brief wave as he peeled off to go to his car.

My car was parked closer to the back of the lot. It was a way to get a few more steps in every day. I dug out my phone as I hurried through the cold.

It rang once before Mom answered. "Hi, honey."

"Hi, Mom." I fumbled with my key fob and finally got the door unlocked. "Can you do me a favor?"

"Of course."

I smiled as I climbed behind the wheel and pulled my door shut. I might have my differences with my parents, but they were unquestionably there for me. Always. "Preston Swift is back in town. I guess his great-grandmother convinced him to help out with the play and get the full experience. He needs a place to stay."

"We'd be happy to have him here."

I started the car. "I'll keep that in reserve. I was wondering if you could check with the apartments first. Or maybe you know of a house that's still free?"

"Hm. That's a long shot."

"I know. I figure students have snapped everything up, but I wanted to check." I started toward the auditorium, mulling over the options. "It's possible he'd buy a house."

"For three months? That's ridiculous."

It was. But then, so was buying a car for three months. A car, at least, he could take with him when he left. On the other hand, he could rent a house out to students and have another income stream, depending on where it was located. Or maybe to faculty.

"It's just a thought. Can you do some research? I'd like to have options."

"Sure. I'll see what's available, but you know it's not likely to be much."

"I do. I have one other idea, but I need to talk to housing about it." I vaguely recalled that two of the residence directors had gotten married over Christmas break. That should mean that one of the RD apartments was empty. Maybe the college would let Preston stay there. In some ways, it'd be the best option if he was really going to get the full Gilead Bible College experience. "I'm headed to auditions. He's coming along. So if you get some info, text or call, okay?"

"Of course. Where's he staying tonight?"

"The hotel is my next call."

"Let me do that for you."

"You don't mind?" I made the turn into the auditorium parking lot.

"Not at all. I'll talk to you soon. Enjoy the auditions."

I smiled at the hint of laughter in Mom's voice. She knew I hated them. But for whatever reason, the college had made attending them part of my job. I gathered the theory was that it would help me sell the play to donors, but I was pretty sure I could've done that without sitting through auditions. Oh well. "Yeah, yeah. Thanks, Mom."

"It's not a problem. Love you."

"Love you, too." I ended the call and parked beside a shiny blue convertible with the unmistakable three-pronged Mercedes logo. Between the fact that I didn't recognize it—I really would have seen a car like that driving around in Gilead, or heard about it—and the temporary tag in the back, I figured it was Preston's.

I grabbed my purse and phone, and hopped out of my car. I peered into the convertible. Preston waved before pushing open his door.

"That's quite the car."

He ran a hand almost lovingly on the top. "Nice, right? I was surprised they had one in stock. Blue, even."

I imagined he'd made the dealer's day. Possibly year. "Not sure how practical it is for the winter here."

"It has a heater." He shut the door. "And it'll be fun to drive home when it's time."

I shook my head. I couldn't imagine driving to Chicago in that thing. "It's like twelve hours."

"Maybe eleven."

"Better you than me." We crossed the parking lot and reached the main doors to the auditorium.

Preston increased his speed and beat me to the door. He opened it and held it as I went in.

"Thanks." I glanced over my shoulder at him as we made our way into the foyer and then through the doors into the auditorium. Inside, I stopped and looked around before gesturing to where the concessions were set up. "Let's go over and I can introduce you to Letty. We have a few minutes before they get started."

"Sounds good." He tucked his hands in his pockets. "You're serious about me helping with food?"

"I'm serious about finding you a way to participate. Isn't that what your great-grandmother wants?" I couldn't stop the slight frown. It wasn't that I cared about what he did. What I cared about was the money for the college. And it was sounding more and more like his great-grandmother was really behind those purse strings. I wanted to be sure they stayed loose and that money for sure flowed.

"Yeah, I guess. But, I mean, what she doesn't know…"

"Nope." I shook my head. "She wants you to help. This is an easy way to do it."

He sighed. "You should be a mom."

I flinched as the barb went straight to my heart, but I quickly tried to cover by clearing my throat. "Anyway, here's Letty."

I hurried the rest of the way to concessions and waved to catch Letty's eye.

"Hi. You want some coffee? Or a snack?" Letty smiled at me.

"No, thanks though. I wanted to introduce you to Preston Swift." I gestured for him to join us. "He's going to be staying in Gilead through the duration of the play and thought he could help with concessions. Can you use an extra hand?"

"Um." Letty looked at Preston. "Have you ever worked concessions?"

He shook his head. "But I learn fast. I know a little about the food industry. I could always work the register or restock. Whatever you need help with."

"I like the attitude. We can give it a try." Letty held out her hand to Preston. He shook it. "Can I get your email address? We'll be having some trainings that you'll need to attend. I can send you details."

"Sure." Preston reached into his pocket and pulled out his wallet. He slipped a card out and offered it to Letty. "All my info's there."

Letty took the card and tucked it away without seeming to look at it.

I reached over and tentatively touched his arm. "Let's go get seats. It looks like the director is getting ready to start things."

I led the way down the aisle a bit before scooting into an empty row. There was a good view of the stage and we were situated near one of the wall sconces, so the light of my phone shouldn't make a discernible difference in the room. I liked to take notes. Sometimes they asked me for my thoughts about casting, so it seemed like I ought to actually have some.

The first several auditions were straightforward. I didn't bother with many notes. There were no major standouts as far as I was concerned. But when I saw the next woman scuffling onto the stage, I cringed.

"What?"

I looked over, startled. "What, what?"

"You look like you're nauseated."

I smothered a chuckle. "You might be too, in a minute. It's Mrs. Plugh."

Preston held his hands up, a questioning look on his face. "Should that mean something to me? She's not famous, is she? I don't really follow Hollywood."

"No. Oh, my, no. She just keeps life in Gilead interesting."

Mrs. Plugh took the microphone and held it too close to her mouth. "I'll be doing a dramatization of Mary, the mother of Jesus."

"From when?" The director's voice was only slightly bored.

I shifted in my seat. He really shouldn't let his disinterest show like that. I tapped a quick note in my phone. The question would be whether or not I could find a way to mention it.

"The cross." Mrs. Plugh's tone implied that it ought to be obvious.

The director's sigh came over the sound system. "Proceed."

"My baby! My baby! Why? Why does he have to die? You did this!" Mrs. Plugh threw an accusing arm at the invisible passersby that she was blaming. "You're killing the Savior of the world, the fruit of my womb..."

"Thank you." The director's voice was sharp. "That's all we need."

Preston covered his mouth as he looked at me, eyes laughing.

I hunched my shoulders. On the one hand, it was pretty hilarious. On the other, it wouldn't be the auditions for the passion play if Mrs. Plugh didn't bring her overdramatic interpretation to the stage.

"Tell me they don't cast her."

I glanced around to make sure no one else had overheard Preston's whisper. No one was looking our way. "Not as Mary. They'll usually offer her some kind of part in the crowd that's not a speaking role."

"Does she take it?"

"Depends on the year." I searched through my memory. The years that Mrs. Plugh went ahead and joined in were some of the more memorable. But not usually for good reasons. "Maybe I'll see if there's a way to recommend we find her a more permanent behind-the-scenes role."

"Not concessions. Please."

I laughed. The sound caused heads to turn my way. I winced and slid down in my seat. "No promises."

I turned my attention back to the stage in time to see the next person approach the microphone. I didn't recognize him at all, which was odd. Usually, in a town the size of Gilead, I could at least place a face. I even recognized most of the students.

The man spoke into the microphone. "I'm auditioning for the part of Judas."

My eyebrows lifted. He actually *wanted* to be Judas?

"Why would anyone volunteer to be Judas?"

I smiled at Preston's whisper since it so closely matched my own thoughts. I shrugged. I couldn't explain it. As I listened to his audition though, I thought he had potential.

As the auditions wore on, I regretted not having taken Letty up on the coffee at the start of everything. I could always head back to the concession area and get some, but at this point in the night it was a bad idea.

Finally, the director wrapped things for the evening and the house lights came up. I stood and arched my back to stretch it. "Well?"

Preston stood, his arm brushing mine. He took a step back before turning to look toward the stage. "You've got some talent trying out."

"And then there's everyone else."

He snickered. "I wasn't going to say anything."

I gestured for him to move toward the aisle, and checked my phone. Mom had come through with a reservation at the hotel for a couple of days. "You're set at the hotel."

"Yeah? Thanks. I could have figured that out." He reached the door and pushed it open, then held it for me.

I slid past him, trying very hard not to make contact with him. Something about Preston Swift made me too aware of... everything. "I didn't want you to get there and find they were full."

"I appreciate it." He tucked his hands in his pockets and stood just inside the doors that would take us to the parking lot. "I guess I'll see you around?"

"What will you do all day while you're in town?" The words escaped before I took the time to think them through.

He shrugged. "Have laptop, will travel."

I nodded and mentally kicked myself. Duh. The man ran a massive family enterprise. Of course he had work. I cleared my throat. "If you get bored and want to meet up to eat, let me know."

"Yeah?"

I nodded again like some kind of ridiculous dashboard spring-headed animal.

He grinned and I could feel myself melting. "Want to meet for lunch tomorrow around eleven thirty?"

"Sounds great." Hopefully, I didn't have any meetings that I was supposed to be at. Normally, my schedule was right on the tip of my tongue. Not around Preston.

That couldn't possibly be a good thing.

Could it?

10

PRESTON

I parked in the visitor spot in front of the college administration building and checked the time, again. I was a little early. Okay, I was a lot early. Wendy had said to meet her at one. It was only twelve thirty. But also? She shouldn't have dangled a surprise in front of me like that.

I'd been meeting her for lunch every day this week. At this point, the people at the diner knew me on sight and I was already developing a usual order. There were two places in Chicago that knew me that well. But I had to admit, I was missing some of the anonymity city living offered.

I swiped open my phone.

It wasn't so cold that I couldn't sit out here until it was closer to time to go in. There was always email to handle. I could do it on my phone.

Mostly.

I'd shot off three replies when someone knocked on my window.

"Aren't you freezing?" Wendy rubbed her arms, her eyebrows lifted to where they almost disappeared under her hair.

I clicked off my phone and pushed open the car door. "It's

not so bad out of the wind."

As if to prove my point, a gust blew icy air past us.

Wendy's hair danced around her chin. There was no reason for me to find that beguiling.

I looked away.

"Come inside." Wendy sounded like her teeth were going to start chattering any minute.

"I didn't want to come in. I know I'm early." I shut my car door and reached into my pocket to click the lock on the fob.

"My meeting ended sooner than I anticipated." Wendy's steps were long as she hurried toward the door.

I lengthened my stride to catch up, and reached for the door handle. I pulled it open and held it as she went in. I didn't miss the look she gave me out of the side of her eye. I couldn't quite interpret it. But I didn't miss it.

There was no reason for it to leave my insides gooey. I wasn't here to find love. Or romance. Or anything like that. I was here to make GG happy by staying through the passion play and helping out with concessions. Then I'd go back to Chicago and get on with my life. And Wendy would stay here in Kansas and get on with hers.

We could be friends in the meantime.

"Much better." Wendy unwound the scarf from her neck and draped it on the coat stand inside her office door. She gestured to the couch on one wall. "Have a seat."

I shrugged out of my coat, dropped it on the arm of the couch, and sat. "I feel like I'm in trouble. Did I do something wrong?"

She laughed. "No. I have a surprise. A good one, I think."

"I like the idea of a good surprise. How long do I have to wait to hear it?"

Wendy grinned. "I should drag it out just on principle. But I won't. I'll start by asking if you're happy at the hotel."

Was I happy at the hotel? How was I supposed to answer that? I wasn't *un*happy there. "I guess? It's a hotel."

"Right. I guess I'm wondering if you're content to stay there until you go back to Chicago or if you'd rather have something else."

"Does anyone actually want to live in a hotel for three months?" Maybe there were people who did. I didn't happen to be one of them. For all that I didn't love the décor in Chicago, it was still home. I could kick off my shoes or hang up a towel crooked and no one had to deal with it except me.

"Mark would have loved it."

I lifted my eyebrows. "Mark is...?"

"My husband." She paused and cleared her throat.

"Right." I'd forgotten his name, which was idiotic. Although, to be fair to me, she hadn't called him by name all that much when she'd given me all the details over fresh pasta.

"It's fine. I shouldn't have mentioned him. Anyway." Wendy made a motion like she was erasing the conversation. "I have an alternative if you're interested. There's a residence director apartment available in the men's dorm. You wouldn't have to be the RD or anything. He and the RD of the women's dorm got married over Christmas break. So they've obviously moved in together. Leaving his place vacant. He's still doing all his duties. He just isn't on site. But if you liked the hotel and all that goes with living in one, I was going to suggest just staying there. We don't have housekeeping."

I chuckled. "I can pick up after myself well enough. That sounds pretty great, actually. Can I see it before I decide for sure?"

Wendy reached in her pocket and drew out a set of keys on a plain ring. "That's why I asked you to come. Do you want to drive over or walk?"

"Let's walk." There was a big part of me that knew I only

chose that option to prolong my time with Wendy. I wasn't going to think about it.

"Really?" She reached for her scarf. "Okay. I figured you'd want to drive."

"It's not far, right?" I stood and put my jacket back on. "I spend a lot of time sitting behind my computer. It's good to walk and stretch my legs whenever I can."

"All right." Wendy gave me a long look before she shrugged. "Let's go."

I fell into step beside her as we made our way back out of the administration building—this time through the doors that opened onto the campus rather than the parking lot. When I'd first arrived, Wendy had given me the tour and pointed out the names of buildings and their purposes, so our walk was quieter.

Students with bulging backpacks hurried around the campus. Others milled around in little groups in pockets of sunshine. It reminded me of my own time in college and I got a little pang in my chest. Did they know these were some of the best years of their lives?

"Here we are." Wendy angled to the left and a walkway that led to one of the taller buildings. "You'll be on the main floor, behind the front desk. And again, you don't have to do any of the RD stuff. Please don't let anyone make you feel obligated."

I grabbed the door and pulled it open for her.

Wendy waited just inside for me, then approached the man at the desk. "Hey, Julian. How are you?"

"Good. Thanks, Ms. Hall. You?"

"So far so good. This is Preston Swift. He might be staying in your old apartment."

"Yeah? Nice. It's a good place. Carol and I almost chose it, but it seemed like the women needed her more often at night than the guys, so it's better for us to be there." Julian shrugged. "You have the keys?"

"I do." Wendy held them up. "You'll help him out, if he needs something?"

"Sure. Of course. Welcome."

I smiled. "Thanks. I'll try not to be a bother."

Julian scoffed. "I can't imagine you'll be a problem. If anything, I feel like I should apologize in advance. We're not exactly quiet around here."

"I remember how it is." Would I be able to get my work done? I'd find out. If it didn't work, then I could move back to the hotel. Or do some of my own scouting for a place to rent. Wendy had told me her mom put out feelers and came back with nothing, but I could always have a realtor do some poking around just in case. For that matter, commuting from Wichita as needed for concessions wouldn't be that bad. Would it? "Nice to meet you."

"Holler if you need anything."

"I will. Thanks."

"This way." Wendy skirted the counter and then back along a short, semi-hidden hallway that ended in a closed door. She put the key in the knob and twisted, then pushed the door open. "Home, sweet home."

I followed her into the space and looked around.

"What do you think?"

"It's great." I was pleasantly surprised. "Brighter and more modern than I expected."

Wendy laughed and it was as if her whole face transformed. All the traces of sorrow melted away. Or most of them did. Knowing now about her husband, I understood a little better why it was there. It just made me want to do whatever it took to make her laugh.

"The furnishings are all owned by the school, so if you find something's broken, just let me know and I'll see what I can do. The bedroom and bathroom are through here."

I ran my hand along the back of the well-loved black leather sofa as we edged around the living room space to the bedroom. This was more spartan. A bare mattress on top of a box spring took up the bulk of the room. There was a standard college dorm dresser. And floor-to-ceiling windows on one wall with blinds pulled to one side.

"Hm." Wendy frowned at the bed. "I thought there'd be linens."

"That's easy enough to remedy. You have a Walmart or something around here, right?"

Her mouth popped open and she stared at me.

"What?"

She snapped her jaw shut and shook her head.

I tipped my head to the side. "I'm serious. What's wrong?"

"I just...you...Walmart?"

I chuckled. "They sell everything I could need from linens to groceries. What's wrong with that?"

"It's not exactly high end."

I shrugged. "Neither am I."

She looked like she was going to say something, but instead she turned on her heel and left the room.

I couldn't help being disappointed. There was something about her snappy comebacks that I looked forward to. That probably said more about me than anything. I made a quick detour to look into the bathroom that connected to the bedroom with, it turned out, another door into the living area. Convenient. Ish.

"It's not a lot. You could maybe find a place in town. Or commute from Wichita. We've had faculty do that." Wendy wrung her hands at her waist. "I'm not sure I realized just how basic the RD residences were."

"They're great. This is great. If I can rent this, I'll be happy."

"Rent?" Wendy frowned. "They don't need you to pay rent."

"Maybe not, but I insist. Seriously, I'll be using electricity. Heat. And they're getting nothing out of me in return like they would with a residence director. Figure out how much or I'll just send in what I think makes sense." I had a feeling that my number would be higher than whatever Wendy came back with. Maybe I ought to handle it on my own. "You know what? Let me do that. Then you can say you told me not to bother and it won't be on you."

"I can't talk you out of it?"

I shook my head.

"All right."

I grinned. "See? Not so hard, right? Now, about that Walmart."

Armed with directions from Wendy and my phone map for backup, I spent the bulk of the afternoon buying what I'd need to make the apartment livable and stocking up on pantry basics. Maybe they'd let me buy meals at the dining hall now and then. I wouldn't mind hanging out and reliving that experience.

Back at the apartment, I worked bedding out of plastic wrappers and pulled tags off towels before throwing them into the washing machine. When the first load was going, I plopped onto the sofa and called GG.

"Preston? Hi, honey."

"Hi, GG." I smiled when she spoke. Her voice would always be a little slice of home. Even if she sounded frailer today than she had the last time we talked. "How are you?"

"Waiting to see Jesus and your great-granddad."

I frowned. "I'd just as soon keep you around. Maybe that's selfish."

Her laugh was quiet and ended on a sigh. "A little. But I'll do what I can. It's not up to either of us. The Lord knows the number of our days. I can be content with that. Are you in Kansas?"

"I am. Just like you wanted. I'm even living on campus."

"You are?" Her voice brightened. "Tell me everything."

I spent the next twenty minutes describing the apartment and the way I ended up here. GG laughed like it was the most hilarious thing she'd heard in a long while. Maybe it was? I didn't imagine nursing homes were the most cheerful and amazing place to live. But that had been her choice, and no one was going to talk her out of it. No one talked GG out of anything.

"Now tell me about this woman. Wendy, was it?"

"GG." I recognized the matchmaking tone in her voice. "She's just the woman who handles donors and development at the college. Nothing else."

"Mmhmm. So she's old? Unattractive?"

"Neither. She's probably my age?" I was thirty-five. Wendy might be a couple of years younger, but she was surely at least thirty?

"And pretty?"

"Every woman is beautiful in one way or another, GG. You told me that." It had been part of a lecture I'd received from my dad and then again from GG when my younger brother Grayson had tattled on me for calling a girl at school ugly.

"So they are. I'm glad you learned that lesson. What makes Wendy beautiful?"

I wasn't sure what to say. There were a lot of things. Physically, Wendy was just the kind of woman I found attractive. She didn't seem to be obsessed with how she looked, and that quiet confidence made her shine. But more than that, her heart—or what I'd seen of it so far—was what drew me. There was hurt there. But she didn't seem to let it define her.

"Oh, my. That's a long pause. Maybe you should just text me her picture and I'll take it from there."

"GG." I shook my head. "Even if I was interested, it's very clear she's not open to a relationship right now. She's a widow."

"I'm so sorry. That's hard. How long?"

"Just over a year, from what I gather. And she lost her girls in the same crash."

GG drew in a sharp breath.

"Exactly." I needed to remind myself of this more often. Despite my protests to GG, I was interested in Wendy. And I'd love to see if there was any chance of dating while I was here. But a relationship with someone like Wendy was never going to be casual. And that caused its own set of problems. I could justify living and working in Kansas for three months to appease GG, but my life was in Chicago. I had to go back. "Beyond that, her whole life is here. Her parents, everything. She's never lived anywhere else. I think at our age, that has to be by choice, don't you?"

"Maybe. Or maybe she just never found the right incentive to leave."

It didn't seem likely that I was going to fill that role. "That's possible."

"I'll pray for you. And for her."

"Praying is good any time. I love you, GG. I don't like being so far away that I can't visit."

"You're a sweetheart. You know I'm fine right here. The doctors say I'm fully recovered from my fall and not dying anytime soon. It makes me happy knowing you're getting a little glimpse of where your great-granddad and I fell in love. Send me more pictures. Okay?"

"Absolutely. Love you."

"Love you, too. Bye now."

I ended the call and set my phone on the couch. My wash was probably ready to shift to the dryer.

And that was a much more productive task than wondering about Wendy Hall.

I stepped through the doors of Heavenly Brew and scanned the small seating area. Monday nights weren't usually terribly busy here, although a coffee shop in a college town never lacked for business. But tonight, a big group of guys had scooted the bulk of the tables together. I frowned as I made my way to the counter.

"Evening. What can I get you?" Letty offered her usual cheerful smile.

"Not sure yet. What's with the gang?"

Letty chuckled. "Jesus and the disciples have gathered."

"Ah." I glanced over again. Duh. Well, good for them. Rehearsals and costuming and all of that were well underway. It was probably good that the various groups who would spend a lot of time onstage together got to know one another. I turned my gaze back to the drink menu. "Can you make me something decaf?"

"That's your only requirement? For here?"

I nodded. I just wanted a reason to sit and be somewhere other than at home. The house was heavy tonight. I'd made dinner and tried to settle in, but phantom footsteps of the girls echoed all around me. And Mark, yelling at them to be quiet. I swallowed. "Maybe a slice of that pound cake too?"

"Sure thing." Letty worked the register.

I paid with my card and moved down to the pickup area to wait for her to work her coffee magic on whatever she decided to put together.

Before long, Letty had put a large mug down on the counter beside a slice of pound cake. "Banana bread cappuccino."

My eyebrows lifted. Unusual. I thanked her and took the treats, then made my way to an overstuffed chair that was pushed into the corner of the shop. I didn't really need a table, anyway.

I sat and sipped the concoction before balancing the mug on the wide arm of my seat. I tucked my purse between me and the arm, dragged my phone out of the front pocket, and opened my e-reader app before breaking off a corner of the pound cake and popping it in my mouth.

I quickly lost myself in the most recent Christian romantic suspense by Tara Grace Ericson. Mom had sent me one of her books last year, and I'd been hooked. I'd been skeptical at first. Romance? Not usually my scene. But Mom had insisted it was just what I needed. In some ways, she'd been right.

In others? Well, I'd always known my marriage wasn't representative of all of them. Look at Mom and Dad. And now my sister, Whitney, and her husband. I could point out many more relationships that had stood the test of time.

So really, who was to say the problem wasn't me?

Mark had certainly believed that was the case.

I sighed and reached for my drink.

"Is this seat taken?"

I looked up. Preston. Of course it was Preston. I forced a smile. "No. Help yourself."

"Thanks." He settled in the other arm chair with a large to-go cup in his hand. "What brings you out on a Monday night?"

"I just needed a change of scene." I shrugged one shoulder. I definitely wasn't getting into the rest of it with him. I'd been doing my best to avoid him for the past week. It had been mostly successful. "You?"

"There's some kind of game night for the guys' dorm in the lobby tonight. It's not conducive to a quiet evening." Preston lifted his cup and drank. "They invited me to join in, but this seemed better. Now that you're here too, I'm glad I begged off. You keep busy."

Had he been looking for me? No one had mentioned it if he'd come by my office while I was out. And someone would have said something. Lissa, the main receptionist, was always looking for gossip. If she'd noticed, she'd probably have the whole town thinking we were on our way to being engaged. "I try to. I like my job."

He nodded. "That's good. It's good to enjoy your work."

"Do you?" I couldn't imagine being part of a family business. Would the expectations be heavy and suffocating?

"You know, I do. But then, Mom and Dad never made it feel like an obligation. In fact, of the six of us kids, I'm the only one who's involved in the nuts and bolts of the company. Some of my brothers do related work, but not all of them."

"Huh. And your family's okay with that?"

"Absolutely. Mom and Dad were big on making sure we pursued God's plan for us, you know? Living off the trust fund was never an option, but beyond that if we used our talents to make a difference in the world, they supported us."

"When you put it that way, I guess my parents did the same. Although the whole trust fund thing was never an option." I smirked at him over the top of my coffee.

Preston chuckled. "I fully admit the safety net is nice. But I like to work. I want to say I'd be doing much the same thing for someone else if I wasn't able to do it as part of Swift Industries."

"Six kids, huh? What's that like?"

"Noisy." Preston grinned before drinking. "Also fun. I have built-in best friends. And maybe Mom wasn't prepared for the twins as the caboose, but I can't imagine not having both of them."

Twins? Twins named Swift. I blinked and tipped my head to the side. "Not *Further Up and In*. Right?"

Preston practically beamed. "That's them. They're great, aren't they?"

I nodded. How had I not even suspected that Preston was related to the guys who made up the Christian band currently taking the world by storm. "They are. There's talk of trying to get them to come play around graduation."

"Yeah? I'll let them know to be on the lookout for it. With the connection to GG, they'll probably do what they can to make it happen. Full-on concert, or more like a chapel?"

I chuckled. "You've got a good understanding of the school already, don't you? Honestly, I think we'd take whatever we could get. Would they want to do both? Friday chapel and then a concert in the evening? I don't know how much is too much."

Preston shrugged. "They love to play. I imagine they'd do both, provided it fits in their schedule. I know they're going on tour in the spring, but I haven't paid complete attention to their plans."

"Do you think if I sent you the contact info for the chaplain's administrative assistant, you'd be willing to reach out and offer an introduction?" I bit my lip. That was kind of a big ask and Preston was already doing so much for the college. The final numbers we'd nailed down for the endowment still made my head spin when I thought of it. The Swift family was going to be the largest donor to the college. And they hadn't asked for anything in return. In fact, it had been somewhat of an uphill battle to get them to allow us to name a scholarship after them.

"Sure. In fact, I can go one better. I'll text Walker tonight with the general idea and have him send me dates that would work. If there are any. Then I can introduce them and they can take over coordinating from there." He sipped his coffee again before setting the cup down on the floor. "How's that?"

"Amazing. Thank you." I shifted in my seat and the plate holding my pound cake started to slide. I grabbed for it at the same time as Preston leaned forward to catch it and our hands touched. I drew in a quick breath, unsure what to do with the sensations sparking on my skin from that brief contact.

For one long, heart-stopping moment, our gazes locked.

I broke the contact and looked away as I rearranged the cake with a murmured, "Thanks."

Preston cleared his throat.

I couldn't bring myself to make eye contact again. "How are you liking the apartment? Are you able to get everything done during the day that you need?"

He paused long enough that I looked over. He was studying me, his expression unreadable. Finally, he answered, "It's great. Definitely quiet enough to get work done. In fact, I find myself putting music on a lot, which I don't normally do when I'm working, because it can get almost too quiet. My admin said she likes me working remotely because I'm less demanding."

I laughed. I couldn't picture him being demanding. In fact, I'd be surprised if his employees didn't consider him a bit of a pushover. "I don't believe you."

"That's what she said. Then again, she was my dad's admin before me, and he was the epitome of laid back. So maybe it's just contrast." He looked down at my lap. "Are you going to eat that?"

"Am I...oh." I held the plate out. "You're welcome to have it."

"Thanks." His boyish grin worked past my defenses, leaving warmth and wonder in its wake. He took the plate, picked up the slice of cake, and took a huge bite. "Mm."

I watched as he made short work of the treat. I drained the last of my cappuccino. Maybe I ought to give it up and go back home. The doctor had prescribed sleeping pills to help on nights when everything got to be too much. I didn't like to take them. They left me groggy and disoriented in the morning, no matter how long I managed to sleep.

"Well." I stood. "I think I'm going to call it."

"You want to take a walk? Or do you need to get back home for something?"

I shook my head. "Nothing pressing. I just...sure. You know what? A walk sounds nice. Maybe on campus?"

"If you like." He stood and gestured for me to go ahead.

I took my cup to the dish return. Preston followed with the plate that had held my—or I guess his—cake. I glanced over my shoulder at him. "Did you drive?"

"No. I wanted to stretch my legs."

And he still wanted to go on a walk with me? It made no sense. Then again, it wasn't as if I knew him all that well. I zipped my coat. "Why don't I give you a ride back? That way, I have my car when our walk is finished."

"Sounds great." He flashed another of his disarming grins.

I ought to be immune to them. He was a donor to the school. Nothing more. The fact that he was here for a few months also shouldn't—didn't—matter. He'd go back to Chicago and I'd stay here, plodding along.

Preston held open the door to Heavenly Brew and I slid past him. I tried not to inhale his warm, piney scent, but failed. Miserably. Just like I failed not to contrast the masculine, woodsy scent Preston wore with the overly chemical spray Mark had preferred. He'd gone on and on about how high end it was because it was by a fancy French designer.

Mostly, it had made me sneeze.

"You all right?" Preston briefly touched my arm.

I'd stopped walking like an idiot. I sent him a tight smile. "Yes. Sorry. Distracted."

"We don't have to walk."

"No. It's a good idea. The air will clear my head." Maybe it would be enough for me to sleep. I wasn't banking on that, but it'd be nice. "I'm parked over here."

We walked in companionable silence to where I'd parked. I unlocked the doors with my key fob as we neared the back of my SUV and I stepped into the street to get to the driver's side. Preston hesitated before continuing on to the passenger door. Had he really been about to come open the door for me? Mark had started out that way, opening doors, holding chairs. He'd been so insistent. Then, when I was used to it, he stopped. And if I paused by a door, he'd berate me for expecting him to do everything. He'd smirk, make his little barbed comments, and chip away at me so subtly at first that I just accepted it. All so I would know he was in charge.

In the car, I started the engine and looked over. He was in the process of fastening his seatbelt. "Your mother must be proud."

He frowned as he glanced up. "She always says so. But why, in this particular case?"

I chuckled. I liked that he was so quick to agree about his mom. They must have the kind of relationship people dreamed of. The one I probably had with my parents, if I was completely honest. They were proud of me. They loved me.

They just didn't always understand me.

My fault, since I kept so much close to the vest. But what good would it do to spill all the details? They couldn't fix it or change it. It would only hurt them more.

"You have lovely manners."

Preston's face reddened. He cleared his throat. "Thanks?"

"It's a compliment. You're welcome. I'm not used to people holding doors. It's nice. You're not weird about it, either."

He snorted. "Good to know."

I hit my turn signal as I came to the stop sign at the intersection that would take us to the college. "Don't act like you don't understand. Some guys make a huge production out of the fact that they grabbed a door. Like you should be amazed at their manliness."

"Hmm."

"What's that mean?"

"Oh. Um. Just trying to think if I know anyone like that. I guess I do. I hadn't thought of it exactly in those terms."

"You're not a woman."

"No, indeed. I am not."

It sounded like both of us were glad that was the case. And really, I shouldn't be. I took a deep breath and reminded myself of all the reasons it was a bad idea to entertain any of the thoughts about Preston that were worming their way into my head.

I didn't respond. I might be rusty when it came to flirting, but that was what this conversation felt like. Or at least it was veering in that direction.

And it shouldn't.

A few minutes later, we pulled into the parking lot in front of the administration building. I took one of the spots near the sidewalk, right under a lamp post, and parked. "Here we are."

I felt him watching me and tried not to look over, but the draw was too much. When our eyes met, I swallowed. The way he looked at me...he shouldn't. And I shouldn't want him to.

"Is this a bad idea?" His voice was quiet, almost a whisper.

I pulled my mental shields closer and tighter around my

heart and forced a cheery smile. It was better to pretend igno-rance than explore anything more. Nothing could work between Preston and me. Or any man and me. I'd had Mark, and that was enough. More than enough. "Why would it be?"

His eyebrows lifted slightly and for just a moment it seemed like he would call me out. Then he matched the cheeriness of my smile with one of his own. "No reason. My bad. Let's walk."

I pushed open my door and got out of the car. There was no reason to be disappointed. His response was exactly the right one. He was only here for a few months. I wasn't looking for romance. And if love was something Preston was hoping to find? Just about any woman on the planet would be a better choice than me.

12

PRESTON

"Happy Valentine's Day, GG." I smiled into the webcam, pleased to see GG looking alert and not as pale as the last time we video chatted.

"Thank you, honey. I got your flowers. You shouldn't have."

"Don't be silly. Of course I'm sending my best girl roses on Valentine's." I'd also sent them to my mom and grandmother. Because it was just something that I did every year. My brothers said I was a suck-up, but it wasn't as if they couldn't send flowers too. Or chocolate. Or any number of things. All three women were special to all of us, and all three of them had lost their husbands. It made sense that the men who remained in their lives should treat them special today of all days.

GG's cheeks pinked. "Did you send flowers to a special lady closer to your age by any chance? That's what would really make me happy."

I'd thought about sending flowers to Wendy and then quickly dismissed the idea. She'd been suspiciously absent over the last two weeks since we took a walk together around campus. I'd thought, for a moment at least, that she was sensing the connection and chemistry between us the same as me.

Apparently, I'd been mistaken. "Well, keep praying about that, okay? So far, God hasn't made it clear who that woman is supposed to be."

"He will. Make sure you're listening."

"I'll do my best. Maybe..."

GG waited a moment before she asked, "Maybe what?"

"Maybe there isn't someone." I shrugged, trying to make it seem like I'd be okay with that. The reality was that I was thirty-five, and, while I'd had a handful of relationships that verged on serious, I'd never felt like God was saying, *Here she is! Marry her!*

"Hmm. I suppose that's possible. I'll pray that you have clarity, one way or the other. I know I hope for you to have the kind of love your great-grandfather and I had." GG paused, held up a finger, and covered her mouth as she coughed. It a was a long, wet, raspy sound that belied how well she looked on camera. "Sorry about that. Are you liking Kansas?"

"GG."

I would've believed the innocence in her expression if I hadn't just heard her cough.

"I'm fine. Promise. Just sometimes get a little winter in my chest." She sighed. "I have enough nurses around here. I don't need you joining their ranks."

I bit back a demand to speak to one of them. It wasn't my place. They'd talk to grandmother. Or even Mom. But me? I was definitely far down the list. And neither Grandmother nor Mom had said anything to me about GG's health. Would they while I was down here? Of course they would.

Right?

I made a mental note to text my brother Cooper and see if there was anything going on.

Grudgingly, I nodded. "All right."

She brightened. "So. Kansas?"

"It's not Chicago."

GG laughed. "No, it's not."

"It's fine. I don't really think I'm being helpful when it comes to the passion play. I'm just working in concessions. In fact, there's training for that this afternoon.

"On Valentine's Day?"

"Yep. I guess Letty asked the other workers what made sense for their schedules, and this was it. It's fine. It's not as if I have plans." I'd wanted them. But, like I'd dismissed the idea of sending Wendy flowers, I'd also not asked if she wanted to have dinner. "Besides, training is only an hour."

"Please tell me you're not eating alone tonight."

I hesitated. Was it a lie to say I wasn't when my plans included visiting the dining hall here on campus? Because I wouldn't be alone. A good portion of the student body would work their way through the lines and congregate at tables at the same time as me. That was the opposite of alone, wasn't it?

"Preston." GG huffed out a breath. It kicked off another coughing fit.

I waited while she coughed, concern growing with every wet, raspy breath. "GG, you don't sound good."

"I'm fine." She looked to her side, and after a moment, sipped from a glass of water. She cleared her throat. "I'll let you go. This is more talking than I usually do is all. But promise me you aren't closing yourself off from the idea of love."

I sighed. "I'm not, GG."

"Okay. I love you."

"I love you, too." I ended the call and set my phone aside. I hadn't lied. I wasn't closed off to the idea of love. It just also wasn't something I was actively pursuing. Until a month ago, it wasn't even something that I'd been considering. The prospects in Chicago all seemed to see me as a meal ticket or a beneficial corporate merger.

I didn't want to be either of those things.

And even though the donation GG was providing to the college was large enough to raise eyebrows and have someone questioning just how many zeros were at the end of our family fortune—if, in fact, they hadn't searched it out online—I didn't get the feeling that Wendy cared. Or, well, not beyond how it benefited Gilead Bible College.

It was refreshing.

I checked the time. Training was at two at the theater. If I walked slowly, I'd make it there in plenty of time without appearing overly anxious. Since I didn't have any pressing work that needed my attention, it seemed reasonable enough. If I happened to take the longer way around and walk past the administration building? So be it. Maybe Wendy would be available for a break.

No. That was dumb.

I tucked my phone in my pocket and bundled up against the winter wind before leaving the apartment and making my way out of the dorm. I hesitated at the end of the sidewalk, then turned right. If I didn't go the long way, I'd be too early. And I sure didn't want to appear eager to learn about working a concession stand.

I snorted.

I was definitely not excited about working concessions.

I slowed my pace and looked around as I walked. Students crossed between buildings in groups or solo. Some carried books. Others had backpacks. Some strolled hand in hand, clearly taking a minute or two to embrace the fact that it was Valentine's Day.

One couple sat on a low wall as close as could be. She smiled dreamily at him for a moment before he slid off the wall to one knee.

I slowed even more, not wanting to gawk, but not willing to stroll on by while an engagement was in progress. The girl clapped her hands over her mouth and squealed as she nodded vigorously. The boy grinned and leapt to his feet, scooping her up in the process.

I chuckled and continued on my way.

Good for them. Hopefully, they'd have a long life together serving God and each other. That was how my parents had always talked about marriage—a journey of serving one another while serving Jesus together. It had worked for them. For my grandparents. And for my great-grandparents. So there had to be something to the idea.

Before long, I made it to the administration building. My cheeks were stinging from the cold. After a brief hesitation, I strode to the doors and went inside.

"Good afternoon, Mr. Swift." The admin greeted me with a curious smile. "Can I help you?"

"Oh. Sorry. No. I'm on my way to concessions training, but thought I'd stop in here and warm up before going the rest of the way." It sounded stupid. I should have gone the other direction. I shouldn't have come in the building.

She shot me a quizzical look, but the phone drew her attention before she could point out what I already knew about the easier way to get to the theater.

I rubbed my hands together and reached for the door.

"Preston?" Wendy hurried down the hall. "I thought I heard your voice."

I let go of the handle and basked in the warmth of Wendy's presence. "Hi."

"You're on your way to concessions training already?" She glanced at her watch. "It's a little early, isn't it?"

"I wanted a walk. It's a light work day." I shrugged. I couldn't explain my restlessness to myself. I was definitely not going to be able to explain it to Wendy.

"Lucky you."

"Busy day?"

Wendy blew out a breath. "Incredibly. But for a good reason, I guess."

I frowned. "What do you mean?"

"We got a new donor. She made a fairly sizable gift. It just feels like it's going to end up being complicated." Wendy shrugged. "So good. But also potentially problematic."

Had my—well, GG's—donation caused the same little line between Wendy's eyebrows to deepen like it was now? Hopefully not. The whole goal was to make things a little easier for the college, not to cause problems. "Can you share why? Or, probably not. I imagine it's confidential."

She nodded, her gaze darting to the side toward Lissa who, despite holding the phone to her ear, was openly hanging on every word we exchanged.

I fought a grin. "That's as it should be. I'll pray that things don't end up being awful. If there's any way I can help, please let me know."

Wendy touched my arm. "I will. Thank you."

It didn't mean anything. So I was going to ignore my body's reaction and take it as the friendly touch she intended. "Any time. Seriously."

"I guess I'll let you get back to your walk. You don't want to be late to concessions training."

I snorted. "I'm not sure why we need training. We give people food and take their money. Is it really hard?"

"It's...a little more than that. Letty takes the food situation pretty seriously. You'll see." Wendy started to turn, paused, and looked back at me. "Are you busy tonight?"

My eyebrows lifted. "Not really."

"Would you want to have dinner with my parents? They're insisting that I shouldn't be alone. Because it's Valentine's Day." Wendy made a face. "I was content to ignore that, but Mom put her foot down and I have a feeling it's going to be this whole thing."

"So I'd be what, like moral support?"

"Something like that. But you know what? That sounds really dumb when you say it. Forget I said anything. I'm sure it'll be fine."

I studied the red blazed across her cheeks. "I'd be happy to come. A home-cooked meal beats the dining hall any day. And your dining hall isn't even that bad."

"Really?"

"Sure. Sounds like it might be fun." That was probably pushing it, but I liked the idea of helping her out. And if I got to meet her parents and get more insight into what made Wendy Hall tick? That'd be a bonus.

"Thank you. I'll pick you up around five?"

"Okay."

"Great. Thanks. Really."

I held her gaze. Was I the only one feeling the connection? If she felt it, she was the master of hiding her response. "My pleasure."

Wendy didn't respond. She simply turned and headed back toward her office.

I reached for the door. Out of the corner of my eye, I caught the secretary fanning herself. I smothered a chuckle and headed back out into the cold. Hopefully, Wendy wouldn't be put off by whatever the gossip mill made of the fact that she'd invited me to dinner with her parents on Valentine's Day.

Put like that, it sounded much more interesting than it was likely to be in reality.

I glanced at my smart watch and hurried my steps. I definitely didn't need to be late to training. Even if I still didn't quite understand why we needed it.

Inside the theater foyer, I recognized Letty from Heavenly

Brew. The three others milling around must be the rest of the concession workers. I was last, but not late.

"All right, everybody! Give me your attention." Letty clapped her hands. "Today I'm going to walk you through the concession stand, show you the equipment, and give you the general lay of the land. I only have an hour with you, so that's probably as far as we'll get. Tomorrow when we meet, I'll start showing you how to use the equipment to make the different items we'll be making."

One of the college-aged boys raised his hand.

"Yes, Marco?"

"You know today's Valentine's Day, right? I mean, some of us have plans..."

I snorted and didn't quite keep my thoughts to an inside mutter. "It's an hour. Not the rest of your life."

Thankfully, Letty ignored my snark and after some brief commentary, walked to the door beside the roll-up window that was, most likely, where food would be served, and unlocked it. I followed behind everyone else, my eyebrows lifting at the vast commercial kitchen. This was a pretty robust operation. I listened, growing more and more impressed as Letty went through all the different things we'd be responsible for preparing and serving.

"This seems like a ton of food. It's just a concession stand. It's like you're serving every food that can be found at the state fair." I bit my lip. Should I not have said anything? But still—did people really expect this much food at a play?

"You're not far off. Sadly, we don't have deep-fried pickles or deep-fried green beans. Man, what I wouldn't give for some fried green beans right about now..." Letty shook her head and gave her attention back to the group in front of her. "We serve thousands of people here, not to mention the people who are working on the play itself. We're not some rinky-dink little concession stand. People come from all over the country to see this Easter play. While the story of Christ's death and resurrection is the focal point of everything we do here, we need to offer the complete package, and having well-planned concessions is just one little piece of the bigger purpose of what we do here. The overall impression that GBC makes during the Easter play helps to attract donors, too, that allow us to continue to minister to people through this play. We all have a part to play."

"Some are for honorable use and some for dishonorable use." I wasn't aware I'd spoken aloud until Letty pointed at me and nodded.

"Exactly. When you look at that passage, you'll see that it's about the body of Christ, right? Each part of the body has a purpose, and not all purposes are glamorous. That's true for the passion play, too. We're not all going to be stars on the stage, but we all have a part to play, and if any of us fall down on the job, the whole body—the play and the people it ministers to—suffer as a result. So we do our job, and we do it well. In doing that, we serve our brothers and sisters in Christ."

I wasn't alone in being inspired by her words. Nor did it seem that I was the only one who hadn't taken the time to think of serving concessions as also serving Jesus. It was so easy to compartmentalize my life into work, play, and serving God when, in reality, serving God was part and parcel of everything I did. Or it should be.

Huh. I glanced at Letty. It was good to be reminded of that.

When Letty seemed to have exhausted her list of foods that we'd be making, I asked, "What about fruit? Or anything healthy? I mean, I know it's a concession stand and fried food is king, but...?"

"Yeah, it doesn't sell as well, but we do that too." Letty sort of waved away the question, as if it was unimportant.

Maybe it wasn't important. If it didn't sell and the point of concessions was to make money—or at least break even—maybe it made sense that it wasn't a focus.

Letty pointed out a few more things, then we all filed out of the concession area. The marching band was just coming through the foyer. They came to a stop as an overwrought woman began shrieking loudly at Letty and claiming to be her mom.

The college kids looked like they wanted to sink into the floor. I couldn't blame them. It was...awkward. And Letty just stood there. Was this woman her mother? Really? Ugh.

I inched backward along with the rest of the team, trying to give Letty some privacy, although that seemed to be the last thing the woman wanted.

Letty spun to face us and reminded us that we'd have more training again tomorrow. She completely ignored the woman—I just couldn't believe she was really Letty's mother—though it didn't seem to register to that woman.

"Mrs. Stanley!"

I glanced toward the raised voice. Dawson? I hadn't seen much of him, which was surprising given how small Gilead was. Then again, he had a job to do. As did I. I glanced at the altercation still going on and started to ease back.

Letty seemed to be done with us, so I could go back to my apartment and do some work until Wendy came to pick me up for dinner.

As I made my way toward the doors, I heard Dawson's voice echoing through the foyer. And the woman—Mrs. Stanley?—responding. She was a donor?

Oh. My stomach sank. It had to be what Wendy was talking about. And if it was? Wendy was right. Complications were definitely headed her way.

13

WENDY

What had I been thinking?

I stared at my computer screen and kicked myself. Sure, I was absolutely not looking forward to dinner with my parents tonight, but had I honestly thought inviting Preston to come was going to be a good way to assuage that situation?

Ugh.

I spent another several minutes trying to figure out ways to get out of taking Preston to my parents' house. It should be as easy as canceling, but it wouldn't be. He'd want to know why. He'd deserve to know why.

I didn't have a great reason. Not one that made any kind of sense. I wasn't going to get into how he made me feel. Not with him. Not with myself.

I was going to continue ignoring the random thoughts of Preston Swift when they popped into my head. I was going to avoid touching him whenever possible so I didn't have to analyze the physical reaction I had to something as simple as shaking his hand.

I certainly wasn't going to let myself wonder what it would be like to kiss him.

I sighed and dropped my head back against the top of my desk chair. At least now I had a new reason for not being able to sleep.

My therapist would probably consider it progress.

I snickered. Maybe I ought to make an appointment and see if I was right. Nah.

I forced my mind back to my work. The recent large donation from Mrs. Stanley still had several steps before it was official. I scowled at my computer. Yesterday, the one time I took some personal time, Lissa had to decide that she's perfectly capable of doing my job for me, despite the robust set of procedures and protocols for big donors that the college established at their very start. And sure, it wasn't complicated. It was entirely possible Lissa would have been capable of setting up Mrs. Stanley's donation for success.

But she didn't.

And she didn't call me. I would have come in. Mostly, I'd spent the day puttering around at home and wishing I could nap. As much as my insomnia seemed to be catching up with me, the exhaustion went away the minute I got in bed and pulled up the covers.

It was infuriating.

Much like Lissa.

I'd found out about it when I came in this morning and had spent the bulk of my time before Preston's brief interruption trying to quickly research Mrs. Stanley to make sure she was the sort of donor the college was going to be happy having listed publicly.

Nothing had popped immediately, but I'd sent out the information requests as usual anyway. If it was quick and easy, then great. But my gut suggested that wasn't going to be the case.

A knock on the door had me glancing up and I struggled to control a wince at the sight of Lissa. It was like I'd summoned her from the front desk with my thoughts. I gestured for her to come in.

"Yes?"

Lissa preened slightly as she handed me a FedEx mailer. "This just arrived. Looks like it might be to do with the big donation I handled for you yesterday. I'm going to talk to Mr. Watersby about adding your duties to mine. There's no reason I can't do them both. Then you'll be free to find something else to occupy your time since we don't need you here."

I offered her a tight smile. The best option was to not engage. I got so tired of biting my tongue around her, but if she was going to talk to HR, then I'd just have to be sure I beat her to the punch. Because the envelope I was holding meant we'd probably be returning that donation and should never have taken it in the first place.

"Thanks for dropping this off. Could you close the door behind you?" It was a little rude, but I wasn't perfect.

Lissa scowled at me before leaving. And closing the door a bit more sharply than truly necessary.

Whatever. It was closed. I opened the mailer and shook out the papers inside. Usually, the board member who did the deeper digging would call or email. For him to send it this way didn't bode well.

I scanned the top sheet and closed my eyes.

Oh, man.

I took a minute to skim the backup evidence that was included before picking up the phone.

By the time I finished all the calls, my head was pounding and I was five minutes past the time I'd said I'd pick up Preston.

Everything in me wanted to text him and cancel. Then I'd text Mom and cancel. And then? Well, I couldn't go home—even though that was definitely what I'd prefer—because canceling would send Mom over to pound on my door until I let her in.

So. Curling up in a ball and ignoring life didn't seem to be a valid option at the moment. Which meant I ought to just go on about my business as planned. Mom and Dad often commented on how they appreciated that I hadn't caught the acting bug like my sister.

If they only knew how much acting was a normal part of my life.

I shot Preston a quick text, letting him know I'd gotten caught up and was on my way, then quickly shut down my computer. I tapped the papers that had been delivered and shook my head before dropping them into one of my desk drawers and locking everything.

I gathered my coat, purse, and keys and, with a final glance around to ensure everything was as it should be, turned off the lights and locked my office behind me as I headed out.

Lissa wasn't one to stay a minute past five, so her desk was blissfully empty as I passed it. I tried to dredge up a smile thinking of how annoyed sweet Mr. Watersby had sounded when I ran the whole situation past him. But losing Lissa, if that was what it came to, would mean someone had to answer the general phone line, and a lot of the administration seemed to think I didn't have enough work to occupy my time. Which meant that was likely to end up being my job, at least temporarily.

But I'd worry about that when—or if—it happened.

I unlocked my car and climbed in. I turned on the engine and quickly shut off the blast of cold air. I'd turn it back on when I'd been moving a while and there was a chance of the air being warm.

It was a short drive to the dorm where Preston was living. I pulled into the circle in front of the main doors and was shifting into Park when the doors opened and Preston hurried down the sidewalk toward me.

He pulled open the door and got in. "Hi."

"Hi. I'm so sorry. We had a bit of an emergency this afternoon."

His eyebrows lifted, but he didn't ask.

I appreciated that. I probably couldn't—shouldn't—get into the details. No matter how nice it might be to have someone to vent to. I cleared my throat. "I appreciate you doing this. Mom likes to have people around on holidays."

Preston chuckled. "Valentine's Day included?"

I eased out onto the street. "Valentine's, Arbor Day, she's not picky. Any excuse to have a dinner gathering. Especially if it means her kids are around."

"I guess she misses your sister?"

I nodded. I wasn't completely sure that was true. Mom and Whitney talked on the phone a lot. Or Scott sent the plane out to pick them up. Or to bring Whitney out. Honestly, we saw more of my sister now that she was married and a mom than we had when she was living in LA trying to make it as an actress.

It didn't take long to get to my parents' place, which was good because our conversation had definitely stalled. Bringing Preston was a dumb idea. I pulled into the driveway behind a car I didn't recognize and parked. "Here we are."

Preston seemed to study the house. "It's homey."

"It is." I looked at the place I'd grown up and nodded. It was homey. And safe. And I couldn't help wishing I'd learned a little bit more about real life while I'd lived here instead of being so sure of myself and ready to go. Maybe then I wouldn't have fallen for all of Mark's lines.

I sighed and got out of the car.

Preston exited his side and met me at the hood. "Everything okay?"

I smiled. "Yeah. Of course. I don't like being late."

The look he gave me suggested he didn't really believe my excuse, but at least he didn't push.

I knocked on the door before pushing it open and calling out. "We're here! Sorry I'm late."

Mom came bustling from the direction of the kitchen as I was showing Preston where to put his coat. Behind her, grinning like she'd pulled off the world's biggest surprise, was my sister.

"I didn't think we'd beat you." Whitney skirted around Mom and flung her arms around me. "Surprise."

I laughed and squeezed her tight before easing back. "Happy Valentine's Day. This is Preston Swift. He's visiting the college and helping out with the concessions while he's here."

Whitney stuck out her hand. "Nice to meet you. Come on in. You should meet my husband."

That was probably true. Preston and Scott would undoubtedly have a lot to talk about, since both were billionaires. I hung back as Whitney dragged Preston toward the living room.

Mom tipped her head to the side. "Long day?"

I nodded and felt tears burning the backs of my eyes. I blinked them away. There was no reason to cry.

"I was hoping this might make Valentine's Day a little easier. A little more fun. You must miss Mark today. And the girls." Mom pulled me into a hug. "We all do."

I swallowed. "I'm trying to move on."

Mom leaned back and searched my face. Whatever she saw must have satisfied her, because she nodded. "Good. That's good. Is Preston helping with that?"

I was helpless to stop the rush of heat in my face, but I shook my head. "He's not—it's not like that."

"Hmm."

"Mom." I closed my eyes and took a deep breath through my

nose. I opened my eyes and waited until she met my gaze. "Please. Let it be."

"All right. You can't blame a mother for trying." She gave me a little shove toward the living room. "Go mingle with your family. Dinner will be ready in five."

I stood in the empty foyer for a minute after Mom left, trying to get my emotions under control. There couldn't be anything with Preston. For a whole bunch of reasons.

Most of all? I didn't need him to go home to Chicago in April and end up heartbroken in Gilead. Again.

14

PRESTON

I sat hunched in the front seat of my car with the engine running, waiting for Wendy to show up for work. I hadn't seen much of her since Tuesday when I'd joined her at her parents' house for Valentine's Day. Deep down, I'd had some half-baked hope that there'd be some glimmer letting me know she felt the same about me as I did about her. And maybe there was? But I could also have been imagining it.

Even still, I'd had a good time. Scott Wright was a neat guy and I was already trying to figure out when I could get out to the DC area to hang out with him and his group of friends. Most of my friends were family. It was always tricky once money entered the scene. I learned in elementary school that there were people who would pretend to be my friend because of what they thought they could get out of me. Maybe I was a little more cautious about relationships because of it, but I didn't want the Swift family name to get dragged through the tabloids because I couldn't see a gold digger when they appeared.

I shifted and sat up as Wendy's car pulled into the parking lot. As usual, she chose a spot toward the rear. I shook my head. I could think of several better ways to up my step count than walking through a freezing parking lot every day, but whatever floated her boat.

When she neared my car, I pushed open the door and got out. "Morning."

She glanced over. "Hi. What brings you out so early?"

"I was hoping we could chat. Maybe in your office?" Her eyebrows lifted, so I tacked on, "It's work related."

"Sure. Come on in. You could have made an appointment and not beaten the birds out of bed."

I hurried my steps as we approached the door. Having shoved my hands deep into my pockets, I now risked one to the cold air and grabbed the handle, then pulled it open for Wendy and followed her through.

I glanced over at the reception desk and was grateful the busybody who normally sat there wasn't yet at her spot.

"She gets in right at nine." Wendy shot me a knowing grin. "Why do you think I come in so early?"

I laughed. "I hadn't thought of that."

Wendy unlocked her office and gestured for me to go in. It grated on my nerves, slightly, to precede her through a door, but whatever.

She closed the door with a quiet click and unwound the scarf she'd wrapped around her neck. "Have a seat and tell me how I can help."

"It's actually how I can help. Or at least how I think I can help."

"Now I'm curious." Wendy moved around her desk and sat. "What do I need help with?"

"Letty's mom?"

"Ugh." Wendy flopped back in her chair, her eyes rolling heavenward. "That woman."

My lips twitched. "I spent some time the past two days in Heavenly Brew, as well as just kind of wandering Main Street.

Bumped into Dawson again. He mentioned the situation and how torn up it's making Letty. I also heard several people talking about how they were sending in donations, but even if everyone gave what they could afford, it probably wouldn't be enough to cover losing the money from Mrs. Stanley. Would it?"

Wendy made a tiny head shake. "I can't get into specifics like that."

"That's what I thought." I winked. I could read between the lines when it came to financial matters. And Dawson had laid it all out pretty clearly to start, anyway. "I'd like to offer a donation equivalent to hers. On the condition that you return her money. I'm already vetted. From what I gathered on the grapevine, there might be some issues with her qualifying as a donor anyway. And I don't want the school—or the play—to suffer. But I'd also like to help Letty out. It's pretty clear she's tried to cut ties with her family for good reasons."

"You'd do that?" Wendy blinked at me.

"I would." All of the reasons I'd given were factual. But I'd left out one other. I was happy to do it just because it might make Wendy's life easier. I'd gotten the impression from dinner on Tuesday that she rebuffed her family's attempts to help. For whatever reason, she didn't seem as reticent to let me in.

Wendy bit her lip. "You've already made such a big donation. Honestly, it's enough that we could give her money back without too much impact."

"I've been praying about this while I was out listening to gossip. I don't want there to be any impact. Letty deserves to be free and clear."

Wendy smiled. "She does. If you're sure, you're helping me out of a tight spot."

"Even better."

She studied me and my heart raced. How was it possible for her not to understand her effect on me?

She pressed her lips together and nodded. "All right. Let's get that started."

I'd been so focused on her lips that her words took a moment to sink in. "Sounds good. This will work, right? It'll give you the ability to return that woman's donation?"

"I'll make sure of it." Wendy's grin was sharp.

I felt a tiny tug of pity for Mrs. Stanley. I had the feeling Wendy was going to enjoy making it clear that no one messed with one of Gilead's people. GG was right. Gilead was something special. Maybe it wasn't where I'd want to live forever, but I was glad I got to spend enough time here to discover what she'd meant.

I glanced at Wendy as she booted up her computer, and my heart thumped.

Maybe that wasn't the only thing I was going to discover.

THE NEXT WEEK passed in a blur. Before I knew what happened —or was in any way ready for it—it was opening night. I'd spent the time during the opening performance working the fryers, since some of the other workers were still unsure about them. I'd gotten a few little pinprick burns when something splashed, but it hadn't been too bad. If I ended up on the fryer every time, I'd probably live, but I hoped Letty kept to her initial promise to rotate us through the stations. The guy working the window had looked like he was having a grand time interacting with the patrons as they placed their orders.

Now, in another surreal turn of events, I found myself in the college dining hall at the opening night after-party. I wasn't sure why I was here, but Wendy had practically dragged me over. And, well, at this point I was willing to do whatever needed to be done if it meant I got to spend time with her.

I glanced over and smiled at her.

"What? Is there something on my face?" Wendy surreptitiously wiped her nose. "I don't know why they put so much whipped cream on these coffee drinks."

"Because whipped cream is delicious. And no. There's nothing on your face." I tried to look away, but my gaze bounced back to her.

Wendy frowned. "Stop staring then. You're making me self-conscious."

"Sorry. Definitely not my intention."

"We should mingle." Wendy reached for my arm.

I let her half-drag, half-lead me through the mass of people gathered. They must have invited everyone who'd done anything for the play to this thing. The crowd rivaled the ubiquitous cast of thousands. I didn't understand how it was possible that this many people were really involved. Then again, I was here and I'd spent the bulk of my time making churros. Not exactly what I would've termed after-party material.

Wendy stopped short, narrowly avoiding bumping into someone. She tipped her head to the side. "You're Dawson."

"Yeah. That's me."

"I'm Wendy, in case you forgot. I'm in charge of fundraising here at GBC. I'm really sorry about what transpired with Letty's mom. I wasn't in the office when Mrs. Stanley came in, or that never would have happened. We have procedures and protocols." She grimaced. "Anyway. I just wanted to thank you for bringing it to Mr. Watersby's attention and for all you did to help rectify it."

Dawson reached his hand out, shaking Wendy's. "No need to thank me. I know it can't have been easy to face that woman and tell her you were returning her money. I appreciate everything you did to help Letty, too."

Wendy gave him a quick nod. "It's always a good day when

doing my job and doing right by a friend go hand in hand like that."

I cast another glance at Wendy. She'd filled me in on the whole drama of Mrs. Stanley trying to buy her way back into Letty's life—something Letty absolutely didn't want—on our way from the play to the after-party. I was grateful to have been able to help make things right.

Before I could chat with Dawson, Wendy was making our excuses and tugging me in another direction. I caught the hint of a knowing smirk on the guy's face as I passed. I would have loved to have gone back and let him know there was nothing between me and Wendy.

Not that I was elated with that being the situation, but I also didn't see it changing. No matter how much I hoped otherwise.

Wendy was good at the schmooze-and-run. We met more people than I was going to be able to remember, and I was usually pretty good at the cocktail party meet-and-greet. But in the situations I was used to, the people I met weren't live animal handlers and iterant cowboys like Penelope and Noah.

Huh. Look at me, remembering names.

I mentally scrolled our path through the crowd as we got in line for some food. Connor was an easy guy to remember, since he was playing Jesus. His face was on a lot of the promo materials. We didn't do much beyond congratulate him on a good opening night before he got dragged off to another conversation. And then there'd been the Australian girl...what was her name?

"Are you okay?" Wendy turned, two cups of punch in her hands, and offered me one.

I took it and sipped. "Sure. It's a lot of names and faces. I was trying to sort them, but I'm not sure I'll remember."

"Seriously? I would have thought this was old hat for you."

I snickered and sipped again as we stepped away from the

table. "You'd think. But the parties I'm used to are a little more...sedate."

She laughed and her whole demeanor changed. What would it take to be someone who got to make her laugh every day? Ugh. What was I thinking? I was only here another month and a half. And Chicago was eleven hours by car.

Of course, I had my own plane.

Her elbow connected with my ribs. "You disappeared again."

"Sorry. What were you saying?"

"I was saying we don't have to stay long if you don't want to. You've been seen. I've been seen. After the big to-do with Letty and the donations, it was important for you to do."

I blinked. "Wait. Why? No one knows I covered the money, do they?"

"It's Gilead." Wendy shrugged. "Word travels. Maybe not above the radar, but there are a good number of people who know or guess."

I frowned. It didn't matter, really, but it wasn't as if I'd done it for credit. Even GG's big donation wasn't tied to naming a building after the family or anything. She just wanted to do what she could to ensure that future generations would be able to experience the same thing she did when she'd attended here.

"I'm sorry. I should have warned you." Wendy looked worried.

I shook my head. "It's fine. Really. I just hadn't thought it through."

"I imagine news still travels in Chicago."

"Yeah. Some." I sighed.

It was different in some ways, but the circles our family ran in had their own gossip mill. Generally, we tried to stay out of them, too. Grandmother and Mom both came down pretty hard on sharing information that hadn't come from the source. My brothers and I could recite the verse in Ephesians about unwholesome talk backward and forward by the time we were ten.

"I still would have made the same decision, so it doesn't matter."

Wendy's expression relaxed into a smile. "I'm glad. Keeping a secret in a small town is nearly impossible."

"Just nearly?" I'd meant it to be teasing, but the way her face clouded, I realized I'd hit a nerve.

"Depends on the secret." Wendy turned away and looked over the crowd. "You ready to go?"

Even if I wasn't, I would have agreed. Wendy was clearly done being there, and I wasn't going to go out of my way to make her life uncomfortable.

"Absolutely."

She shot me a grateful look and we wound through the throngs, pausing when necessary to make our excuses. Outside, I drew in a deep breath of the crisp, cold air.

"It was stuffier in there than I realized." Wendy copied my inhale.

"Yeah." I looked over at her. "Why don't I walk you to your car?"

"You don't have to do that. It's Gilead. More than that, we're on campus. And we're practically at your dorm. I'll be fine."

"Nope. Come on. My mother would kill me if I let you walk to your car alone at night."

"She doesn't have to know. It's cold. Go." She gave my arm a little push.

I captured her hand and gave it a gentle squeeze. "I wasn't really asking. Come on. I'm walking with you."

Wendy pressed her lips together but she didn't say anything. She just turned and started to walk. I fell into step beside her.

"Where *did* you park?"

She glanced over at me. "By my office."

I laughed. "Of course you did."

"I like to walk. And the lot at the theater fills up."

That was reasonable. Although there was a side lot reserved for people involved in the play that she could use. Probably. That said, I'd walked over myself. There didn't seem to be a point to driving the short distance.

Wendy huffed out a breath. "You know, the whole chivalrous thing turns into controlling and borderline abusive when you won't take no for an answer."

I stopped mid-stride, my jaw dropping open. What? How was that even—wow.

Wendy had continued her long, angry strides in the direction of her office without seeming to notice I wasn't with her anymore.

What was I supposed to do? I certainly didn't want to come across as forcing myself on her. I cringed. Just the idea that I was somehow coercing her into something against her will nauseated me. All of Mom's training—and Grandmother's, and GG's, for that matter— warred with Wendy's words echoing in my head.

At the point where the sidewalk intersected with another, Wendy stopped. She glanced to her side and I could almost see the wheels in her head churning when she turned. Hands on her hips, she glared at me.

I held up my hands. She wasn't pointing a weapon at me, but it sure felt like her gaze was lethal.

She was too far away for us to have a normal conversation. And I wasn't going to yell to fill the distance. But I also wasn't sure about moving closer, lest she have another accusation to toss my way.

"Are you coming or not?"

I didn't have to be close to hear the annoyed anger in her voice. I shook my head. "I guess I'll pass. Have a good night."

Her snotty, "Whatever," as she turned and started back on her way to her car summed up my thoughts eloquently enough.

I watched her for another minute before turning toward my apartment. There was part of me—a big part of me—that wanted to follow her and make sure she got there okay. But if walking her to her car was controlling and abusive, following her definitely crossed into creepy territory.

I scowled. Women were ridiculous and not worth the time men spent trying to figure them out. Here I'd thought we were inching our way toward something we both felt. Some kind of relationship. In reality? I guess I'd let GG's tales of romance and GBC get to me and I was seeing feelings where none existed.

I pulled open the main door of the dorm and nodded to the RD at the desk as I moved past him to my apartment door.

Maybe now that the play was underway and I'd been around it and seen how spectacular the production was, GG would be okay with me heading home.

Because I was about done with everything Gilead, Kansas, had to offer.

Up to and including Wendy Hall.

15

WENDY

I glanced over as Mom grabbed my arm.

"There you are. I was beginning to wonder if you'd decided not to come to church today."

I fought the urge to roll my eyes and instead smiled at her. "You know me better than that, Mom."

Mom studied me. "You're not sleeping again."

I sighed. "I'm fine."

"I never said you weren't." Mom slipped her arm through mine. "Come sit with Dad and me."

I wanted to protest. I fantasized, for just a moment, about yanking my arm free and heading home. Instead, I offered another smile that I didn't feel and let Mom lead me into the already filling sanctuary and the spot that Dad had claimed. Always the same spot, week after week.

Someday, some visitor was going to sit in Dad's seat and I wasn't sure what would happen. More than likely, Dad would just choose somewhere else and send fulminating glares in the direction of the interloper. Dad wasn't one to seek out conflict. Until he was. And then? He could be fierce.

I'd only seen it two or three times in my life. And I'd prefer to forget all of them. Of course, if I'd paid attention better at the time, maybe I would have been willing to acknowledge the red flags Mark took pride in waving when he thought no one was paying attention.

I sighed.

Mom glanced at me, her eyebrows lifted in query.

I shook my head and offered a weak smile.

She probably would have spoken, but the worship team took the stage and invited us all to stand. I was glad.

Thinking about Mark was never productive. Talking to Mom about him was even less likely to be useful.

I let my gaze wander over the seats in front of us as I sang and stopped when I recognized the back of Preston's head. Or, at least I thought it was him. He'd joined us a few times since he'd been here. But I hadn't seen him since the cast party. Or, well, technically since after the cast party.

Not that I'd been looking. Much.

If I'd gotten more food than I would normally purchase during the Saturday matinee, it hadn't been because I'd been trying to see Preston. It wasn't as if I needed to see him. Or speak to him. The donation aspect of his relationship to Gilead Bible College was finalized. So, really, he was just here to make his great-grandmother happy. And hey, good for him. He was only here for six more weeks, then he'd head back to Chicago and his fancy billionaire life and I'd be here.

I swallowed as an enormous lump formed in my throat at the prospect of my future stretching out in front of me. Eternally the same.

Because nothing changed in Gilead.

Ever.

Mom tugged my sleeve. I glanced around and hurried to sit as the pastor took the stage and called us to pray together.

My face burned and I forced myself to focus on his words

while asking God to keep me from getting distracted. And to stop obsessing about Preston.

I was able to mostly pay attention the rest of the service. If my gaze darted his way once or twice. I could justify it to myself as just looking around.

After the benediction, Mom turned to me with a smile. "Should we invite Preston to lunch?"

"That's up to you. I think I'm going to head home."

She frowned. "Wendy."

"I've got a headache, Mom." It wasn't a lie. The throbbing behind my right eye had started about halfway through the sermon. I'd started getting migraines after the crash, an oh-so-lovely remnant of the TBI and coma, according to my doctors. I had meds that helped some. But they were all at home along with what helped the best—my bed and a dark room.

Mom's hand gently cupped my cheek as she studied my face. "I've been praying those would go completely."

"I know. I appreciate it. I don't get them as often." They were still more frequent than I'd like, but for the first several months they'd been almost constant. Now I was down to one or two a month. Unless I got too stressed. "But I want to get home before I shouldn't be driving."

"Of course." Mom leaned in and kissed my forehead. "I'll come check on you later."

"No. Mom. You don't need to do that. I'm a grown woman. I'll be fine."

Mom pressed her lips together, but she nodded once.

I reached out and squeezed her hand. "I'll text you later, okay?"

"All right."

I leaned forward to look at Dad. "Bye, Dad."

"Bye, hon. Feel better."

I waved. I'd thought he wasn't paying attention, but apparently that was incorrect. Sneaky Dad. At least Mom had given in without a fuss. I didn't feel like arguing with her. Or anyone.

I must have looked like I hurt, because I made it through the crowd and out to my car without too many interruptions—all blissfully short. In the silence of my car, however, I couldn't keep up the fight against the memories of Mark.

He'd had no patience for illness—not for me or for the girls. Thankfully, he'd never taken it out on them. My shoulders hunched as his words echoed in my mind.

You're coddling them. How do you expect them to cope in the world if you let them skip school like this? And you took off work? Because you think my money's enough for us all, right? Well, good luck. I'll expect to see your half of the expenses deposited in the joint account on time, no matter how many days you miss because you're taking care of the girls. If you'd given me boys like you should have, we wouldn't have this problem.

I swallowed the bile that rose in my throat. My voice came out as a whisper. "Jesus, please help."

The memories quieted, leaving an intensifying pain in my head in their wake. Lights flashed and danced in my vision as nausea twisted my stomach.

Great. Perfect. A full-blown migraine was just what I needed.

A tear slipped down my cheek as I pulled into my driveway. I shut off the engine, grabbed my purse, and hurried as fast as I could to the door. I barely remembered to turn the lock behind me before trudging upstairs, crawling into bed, and dragging the covers over my head.

The blissful darkness enveloped me.

I was groggy when I woke.

The dark felt different, too. Deeper. Heavier.

How long had I slept?

I turned my head to the side and squinted at the glowing red numbers on the alarm clock across the room. Nearly five? No wonder it was dark in my room. There wasn't as much light outside for the blackout curtains to block.

I rubbed my eyes and took stock. My headache was gone, leaving in its wake sluggish thoughts and a sort of echo of remembered pain. I called it the migraine hangover. Mom always tsked at me when I did. She was of the generation that believed Christian girls didn't know about hangovers, let alone joke about them.

In my admittedly limited experience with the alcoholic version, it was still a pretty good description.

I forced myself to a sitting position and, when nothing seemed likely to fall apart on doing so, slipped my legs over the edge of the bed and stood. I brushed aimlessly at the wrinkles in my shirt as I shuffled to the bathroom.

The light was too bright and I squinted against it as I splashed water on my face to try and clear the cobwebs a little better.

I should have changed before crawling into bed.

I smoothed wet hands over my hair, for all the good it did. With a shake of my head, I turned and headed back out and downstairs. I'd dropped my purse just inside the door, and now I fished my phone out of the front pocket and swiped down to see the notifications. Knowing Mom, there would be a couple of texts and at least one call.

It rang even as I held it. I sighed and answered. "Hi, Mom."

"Hi, baby. How are you feeling?"

"Better. I just woke up." Hopefully that would stave off any invitations to dinner. And any suggestions that she come over.

"Will you be able to sleep tonight?"

I thought briefly of the sleeping pills I still had in the medicine cabinet and just as quickly dismissed them. "Probably."

"Hm."

"What's that mean?"

"Nothing. I worry about you." Mom paused, but I could tell she was actively trying to figure out the best way to say something she was sure I'd dislike.

"Just say it, Mom." I meandered into the kitchen and stared at the fridge. I should eat something. I didn't want anything, though. I turned to the pantry and scanned the shelves for soup.

"Your father had a conversation with Preston after church."

"Oh?"

"Well, it's just that he seems like such a nice man. And I know after Mark, it might be hard to find someone who truly compares, but I just don't think it's right for you to decide you're going to be alone for the rest of your life."

I closed my eyes and rested my forehead on the pantry door. "Mom."

"I'm not saying you have to marry him tomorrow. But it wouldn't hurt you to see if there's a chance for something there. I know you'll never forget Mark and the girls. None of us will. But that doesn't mean you can't have something just as perfect again."

I shuddered, grateful she couldn't see me. "I don't want—"

"Wendy."

I pressed my lips together to cut off any retort. There was no purpose in arguing. I would never tell Mom and Dad the truth. Not now.

"Promise me if he asks you out, you'll go."

I weighed my response. After our last interaction, it didn't seem overly likely that Preston was going to be knocking on my door again any time soon. Maybe it was a promise that was safe enough. "Fine."

"Really?"

The surprise in Mom's voice made me smile in spite of myself.

"Really. But don't get your hopes up, all right? He has six

weeks before he heads home. And that's assuming he even stays the full run of the production. It's not as if Letty doesn't have extra workers who could fill in for him if he decided to cut out early." Maybe I ought to find a way to mention that, off hand, to him. Sort of a nudge back to his life.

"Six weeks is plenty of time. Just look at your sister."

I snorted. Mom and Dad hadn't been as gung-ho about Whitney marrying her husband after three months of knowing each other when it was happening. But now, they acted like they'd orchestrated the whole thing. If my marriage to Mark had taught me anything, it was that people could hide their true selves much longer than I ever expected. On the other hand, my marriage to Mark had also taught me that God truly walked with me in the darkest times.

Even if I was only there because I hadn't listened to His warnings in the first place.

"Are you sure I can't bring you dinner? I have a casserole in the oven and there's plenty."

"I'm sure. I'm going to microwave a can of soup and watch a movie. Thanks, though. I love you."

"I love you, too." Mom drew in a breath. I tensed. Was there more coming? "I'll talk to you tomorrow."

We said our goodbyes and ended the call. I blew out a breath and reached for the chicken noodle.

Had I really just promised to go out on a date with Preston Swift?

I wrinkled my nose. Technically, I guess I had.

But he had to ask me out first, and that was never going to happen now.

I tried to convince myself that the sparking of my nervous system was relief.

But I knew better.

16

PRESTON

I shut down my laptop, grabbed my phone and coat, and headed toward the apartment door. I'd gotten in the habit of a walk around campus after I finished my work for the day. Not that my work was ever really finished. I tended to check email and take calls after supper and into the evening as needed. I'd never done that in Chicago. Then again, in Chicago, I had my brothers. My family. And wasn't it hilarious that I missed them like I did? When I'd gone off to college, I'd craved the distance from all of it. I'd even toyed with trying out different majors in hopes of finding a way to get out of the family business. But that was never going to happen. Swift was more than my last name—it was my birthright. I'd embraced that quickly enough, but even back home I guess I took the guys and Mom for granted.

Here in Kansas, I had nothing—it made the reality of what was in Chicago stand out like light against the dark.

I'd thought there might be a hint of possibility with Wendy Hall, but she'd stomped on that pretty thoroughly a week ago. And in case I'd had any lingering questions about the possibility, the fact that she'd managed to stay completely out of sight for a week made her stance on the matter clear.

No matter what her father had mentioned on Sunday.

I chuckled. Mr. Hall was a nice guy. I would have enjoyed getting to know him more. Under the circumstances, it didn't seem like the smartest idea. If Wendy was so determined to avoid me that she'd changed her routines and on-campus exposure, I certainly wasn't going to show up on her parents' doorstep for a home-cooked meal.

I pushed through the main doors of the dorm and blinked against the sun and wind. The days were getting longer with every passing week, making my walks in the afternoon more enjoyable. And somewhat warmer.

I swiped open my phone and tapped on Cooper's contact. I started out toward the theater while it rang.

"Hey, bro." Cooper's voice echoed slightly.

"Am I on speaker?"

"Yeah, I'm hanging with Gray at his place."

"Hey, Pres!" Grayson hollered.

I grinned and pictured them in Grayson's living room, a bowl of chips on the coffee table and some sort of sports-related game on the Xbox displayed on the enormous TV. "Even better. What are you playing?"

"What makes you think we're playing?" Cooper's voice held a hint of affront.

"Aren't you?" I nodded to a group of students as I passed. Faces were becoming recognizable because I took this circuit so often.

"Of course we are." Grayson laughed. "Madden."

I shook my head. "I don't understand why you play football on the Xbox. You could just go get a group of friends together and actually play football if that's what you wanted to do."

"Uh. It's minus two with the windchill right now. No one's playing football today." Cooper scoffed. "Also? I don't want to get hurt. You know I'm a klutz."

There was that. None of us were incredibly athletic. Mom and Dad had, thankfully, never minded. Granddad might have been a tad frustrated, but we didn't mind watching sports with him, so it had worked out.

"All right. That's fair. It's a little warmer here, at least."

"How's Kansas treating you? And when do you come home?" Grayson's voice was louder. He must have moved closer to the phone. Or the chips.

"I'll be home for Easter." The words popped out. I hadn't consciously decided that—but it felt right. The last performance of the play was Good Friday. There was no reason to hurry home. But there was also no reason to stay. I could probably get a couple hours of driving in that night—especially if Letty would let me leave at intermission. Or maybe I could skip the final performance all together and leave sooner. I'd have to ask if that would be all right.

"Nice. It's not the same without you around."

"Aw, what's wrong, Coop? Mom making you actually work in the office?" Cooper worked hard, but he preferred to do it at home. I never minded going in. I liked the vibe of the hive of busy people all focused on the tasks that made the family business what it was.

"You joke, but you know I hate that." Cooper sighed. "And with you out of the office, I'm getting my ear filled with all the petty little complaints. You know how it is."

"I do." I frowned and stopped at the corner to check for traffic before crossing the street. "Although I wasn't aware we'd been having issues."

"I'm handling it."

Grayson snorted.

I bit my lip. It wasn't that I didn't think Cooper could handle it. I just wasn't sure I'd be on board with his choices on *how* to handle it. "Could you maybe shoot me a quick summary email? Just so I'm on the same page?"

"Yeah, I guess. I don't know how you deal with all of that on top of your workload."

"I like it. Do something you love, and you'll never work a day in your life, right?"

Grayson laughed so hard I pictured him spitting chip crumbs all over.

Cooper sighed.

Uh-oh. "What's going on, Coop?"

"I don't know. I love working for Swift. I'm just not sure where I am is the right fit. I don't like pushing paper around, you know?"

My eyebrows lifted and my mind started to sort through alternatives. "I'm not sure I can do anything about it from here. Can you hold on till after Easter?"

"Yeah. Of course. I'm not unhappy."

"But you're not happy."

I waited, but Cooper didn't deny it. Had this been part of what was behind his general dissatisfaction that I'd sensed at New Year's?

"You know Mom and Grandmother would understand if you did something else. Right?"

"I do. They're proud of the twins for doing their own thing. And Gray."

"Why am I always the afterthought, after the twins? I'm older than them." Grayson sounded aggrieved. "Just because I'm not taking the Christian music circuit by storm."

"That's probably something to do with it." I shouldn't tease Gray. He was sensitive about the fact that, while his books sold okay, they weren't hitting bestseller lists, so he was still in charge of the social media for Swift. He didn't do it all. He had a whole department, but I knew it was his dream to make enough to write full time. And he could do that whenever he wanted if he tapped his trust for living expenses, but that wasn't how we'd been raised. "Sorry."

"No. It's fine. I shouldn't be so sensitive." Gray blew out a breath. "Maybe I should come down and visit. See if Kansas has something for me. You sound rested."

"Probably because there's nothing much to do other than work and rest." I grinned and turned onto the sidewalk that would take me toward the dining hall. It was a little early for dinner, but they'd be serving. Might as well stop in, since I was out and about. "But I'd love it if you came. In fact, I've been toying with flying out to Virginia to visit this guy I met briefly. You could tag along and make it less weird."

"How would me being there make it less weird? Not that I mind a trip. I can work from anywhere just like you."

I chose my words carefully, not wanting to get into the whole Wendy thing any more than absolutely necessary. My brothers would tease me mercilessly if they got wind of her calling me controlling and dumping me—which wasn't the right term, it wasn't as if we were together—but it had felt like being dumped, so I was going with it.

"Wendy Hall is the Director of Development here at the college. Her sister, Whitney, is married to Scott Wright. They were in town recently and Wendy introduced us since Scott and some of his friends recently became billionaires. I guess she figured people with money should all know each other? Anyway, he seems nice and down to earth."

"That's rare. Definitely worth developing a friendship." Cooper chimed in. "Maybe I'll come, too."

"Yeah?" I grinned. Just the thought of seeing the two of them lifted my spirits. "Even if we don't fly out to DC, just having you two here would be great. I can get you tickets for the play. Probably. You heard Logan Miles is cast as Judas, right?"

"Nah, man. You missed mentioning that. Think I could meet him?"

Grayson had been a big fan of the guy since his first movie. Usually, he followed any of the tabloid stories where Logan Miles was concerned, so I was surprised Gray hadn't seen the recent article about him and his female friend—the Aussie girl I'd met briefly at the cast party—here in Kansas. "I'll see what I can do."

"Sweet." Grayson cleared his throat. "You want to fly up and get us, or should we book commercial?"

"Fly into Wichita. I'll drive over and pick you up. I left my plane in Illinois when I came down. Made the most sense at the time." I didn't regret the choice every day, but there had been moments. Being able to get home in a couple of hours would have been nice. Even if it was just so I could hang out with my brothers in person rather than on the phone. "Text me your details when you've got 'em. You think you can make it this weekend?"

"That's kind of fast, but we'll try."

I tugged open the door to the dining facility and stopped inside the space between the outside and inside doors. "Just keep me posted."

"Sure thing. Make sure you get us a meet with Logan Miles though, okay?" Gray's voice held enthusiasm. It was good to hear. I'd figure out how to get that meet-and-greet, for sure.

"Will do. See you guys." I ended the call. I breathed in and tried to parse the smells. Something was rich and meaty. Maybe beef stroganoff? I'd gotten better at figuring out what sort of dishes they could serve that would be easy to make in large quantities and keep warm during serving hours.

I dug in the pocket of my jeans for my wallet and fished out the ID the school had issued me when I'd paid for a meal plan. They hadn't known how to handle a short-term plan—it wasn't something they did, usually—so I'd gone ahead and paid for the whole semester. It wasn't a big deal to me, and the lady in the registrar's office had been so flummoxed by my request initially, I'd wanted to put her out of her misery as quickly as I could.

"Evening, Mr. Swift."

"Hi, Kara. You really can call me Preston."

"Oh." Her face reddened and she took my ID card to scan. "I don't think I can. But thanks. Enjoy dinner."

I took my card back and put it in my wallet. "Is it beef stroganoff?"

Kara nodded. "Sure is. It's pretty good. They have apple crumble for dessert. Save some room for that. And put a little vanilla soft serve on top. That makes it even better."

"I'll do that." How long had it been since I'd had apple crumble? GG used to make it. Had she gotten a taste for it here? No, I vaguely recalled her mentioning it was her mother's recipe. Still, I was going to take a picture of it and send it to her. Maybe it'd be a little glimmer of cheer for her.

I grabbed a tray and made my way through the serving area. There were a few students having an early meal, but it was nothing like the crowds I was used to at five thirty. Maybe I'd shift my schedule and eat early more often. It was pleasant to take a minute to consider options without getting my elbow jolted.

On the other hand, it was almost quiet. Early diners weren't full of complaints about their classes or relationship drama. And I'd been greatly amused many evenings listening in as the students bemoaned their days—it was a nice reminder of when life really had been as simple as running behind on an assignment or needing a date for movie night.

Not that my life was overly complicated. Usually. I hadn't had significant relationship drama in years. Until recently.

I found a small table tucked away in one of the far corners of the dining hall and sat. I took a minute to pray over the food and ended up asking God—once again—for direction with the Wendy situation. I couldn't shake the feeling that there was something more there. Even if we didn't end up in a relationship, I wanted to help her.

Maybe all she needed was a friend. I could be that.

I was halfway through my meal when a shadow fell across the table. I glanced up and my heart skipped a beat. "Hi."

"Hi." Wendy looked away and cleared her throat. "Could I join you?"

I glanced around. There were plenty of other empty tables. And the reality was, I'd never yet seen Wendy eating in the dining hall. "Be my guest."

Her lips quirked and she set her tray down.

I glanced at the tiny salad and glass of water. "That's it?"

"There's apple crumble."

"Is that supposed to explain something?" I dug up another bite of gravy-laden noodles. "The stroganoff is pretty good."

Wendy wrinkled her nose. "I don't like mushrooms."

I shook my head. "You're missing out. You don't like the other options either?"

She shrugged and loaded a fork with salad. "Vegetables are good for you. Also, I'm not super hungry. I owe you an apology."

My eyebrows lifted. "Was that the apology?"

Her face flamed red. "No. I'm sorry I snapped at you."

"I forgive you." I tipped my head to the side and considered a moment. "Would you like to explain why you did?"

Wendy's mouth opened and she drew in a breath. She closed her mouth and pressed her lips together before blowing out. "Not really."

"Okay." I wanted to push. But I also didn't want her to dig in her heels. Or call me controlling again. "Do you think I could introduce my brothers to Logan Miles?"

She blinked at me. "Your brothers?"

"Yeah. Cooper and Grayson are going to come down and see the play, hang out a little. Hopefully this weekend, but if not, next. Gray's a big fan of Logan's. I told him I'd see if I could get him a chance to say hi. Maybe get an autograph."

"I don't see why not. I'll talk to the director about some backstage passes for after the performance. It'd be good if you can tell me which one though." Wendy set her fork down. "Are you really not going to demand an explanation?"

"I'm really not. Let's say Saturday night. But if they're not able to get a flight, I'll let you know." I took a long drink of lemonade. "I'm not going to be out of luck scoring some tickets for them, am I? The play is always packed, but it hasn't looked sold out."

"The report I saw this afternoon said there were still about seventy-five tickets for Saturday night available. You should probably get online and buy them tonight, just to be sure." Wendy drummed her fingers on the table. After a moment, she straightened, as if she'd made a decision. "I was going to leave my husband."

I didn't know how to react to those words. Given the accusations she'd tossed at me, I could guess at why—and it wasn't because he insisted on opening doors for her.

My silence didn't seem to faze her. "He didn't know. I was going to wait until after Christmas. One last Christmas for the girls to remember their family whole before their world exploded."

"I'm sorry." It was lame, but it was all I could come up with.

"Don't be sorry. I should have left years ago. Before the girls. I knew better than to marry him. I fought the Holy Spirit on it— I was so determined that it was going to be okay and I was going to have an important husband and I ignored all the warnings, all the reasons to stop." She paused and took a drink. "So it's my own fault. Maybe I deserved it. Maybe it was God's punishment."

"I don't think any of those things are true." I rubbed my hands on my legs. "We have consequences when we go away from the way God's leading us, sure. But I also know He'll use everything in our lives—good and bad—for His glory if we let Him."

She nodded once. "I guess I can be a cautionary tale, if nothing else."

"That's not what I meant." I frowned down at my food. Was I bad at talking to her, or was she determined to misconstrue everything I said? "I'm not trying to be dismissive."

Wendy waved away my words. "I know. I'm sorry. I guess I'm still kind of mad at God. And I shouldn't be. I didn't want to be divorced. I didn't want to lose my girls—because there's no way Mark would have let me have any sort of custody."

"But—"

"He really was a textbook abuser. So charming and wonderful. No one would have believed me, so I never bothered trying to do anything about it. His parents could, mostly, keep him in check. I'd hoped that they would be involved with the girls. Protect them. And maybe I would have been able to keep them. I'm speculating. But I spent most of the six months before the accident praying for a different way. Anything that would keep me from being a divorced failure." She reached for her water and drank. "And I got what I asked for."

"But not what you wanted."

She shook her head and shrugged. "I guess I need to learn to be more specific."

"I'm so sorry." There really should be some other words to say—but what were they? I couldn't help. Couldn't fix this.

"My point—because I got off track—was that I overreacted

to what I know was genuine concern for my safety. And I'm sorry." She stabbed up more salad.

"I appreciate it. Like I said, you're forgiven. And understanding a little more about the why behind it helps."

Of course, it also opened up new problems. Because I didn't have the first idea how to go about wooing a woman who came from that. Was it even something I should do? She'd lost her family a little over a year ago. Even if things had been good, it might still be too fast to move on. Did the truth of her prior situation change that?

"You're thinking hard."

I forced a smile. "Nothing important. I think I'm ready for apple crumble. Do you want me to get you some?"

"Sure. You're putting ice cream on it, right?"

I nodded. "Kara—at the desk?—told me it was the only way."

"She's right."

I took my glass of lemonade off my tray and set it on the table then picked up the tray. I swung by the dish return conveyor belt and set my tray on it before angling back toward the serving area. A line was starting to form for the main dishes. I scooted past and went straight to the dessert area to snag two bowls of apple crumble from under a heat lamp. The smell of cinnamon and toasted oats made my mouth water.

I turned and surveyed the space. I hadn't paid attention to the location of the ice cream machines, because who ate ice cream when it was cold outside? My brother Cooper would say there was no wrong temperature for ice cream, but he was weird about a lot of things.

Aha. I went to the machines and waited for the two people in line ahead of me to finish before adding a generous swirl of vanilla to both dishes.

I made my way back to the table. Wendy had finished her

salad in the short time it took me to come back with dessert. I set a bowl at her elbow and took my seat.

"Glad to see you aren't skimpy with the ice cream."

I laughed. "I figured you'd either be okay with it, or I could scoop some off into my own. I never know with women. Mom and Grandmother both go through phases of talking about how they watch everything they eat. But then they have these huge splurges and seem to enjoy talking about how they shouldn't have."

Wendy grinned. "You've cracked our code. I'm pretty sure that means automatic placement on some kind of hit list."

"If I promise not to tell anyone, do I get to live?"

She shook her head, sighing heavily. "I don't know. Women can't afford to have their secrets getting out like that."

I scooped a bite, enjoying the banter. It was a good change from the explanation about her home life before. "You could put in a good word for me."

"Hm. You've done a lot for GBC. I guess I can try." She took a big bite of dessert and leaned back in her chair. "I should run. Thanks for letting me join you. And for understanding. I guess I'll see you around."

I stood as she did. She sent me a look, one eyebrow raised. I shrugged. Old habits were hard to break, and GG had been insistent on good manners. As had Grandmother and Mom. There were speeches I could probably recite verbatim, but it boiled down to the same thing Uncle Ben had told Peter Parker when he was just figuring out he was Spiderman. In our case? Big gobs of money brought along big gobs of responsibility.

Manners was just part of it.

She pointed a finger at me. "Don't forget to buy your tickets tonight. I'd hate for your brothers to miss out."

She'd turned and was walking through the tables toward the exit before I could respond. I eased back down into my seat, glanced over at her barely eaten dessert, and poked at my own ice cream with my spoon.

I'd spent so much time this week trying to put Wendy Hall out of my mind. Now? She was more deeply lodged in there than ever.

17

WENDY

I brushed a hand nervously down the side of my slacks. Why had I come out tonight? It wasn't as if I hadn't seen the play hundreds of times—literally hundreds—in my lifetime. Even this year I'd already been twice. And yet, here I was.

I'd convinced myself that I needed to hand Preston the backstage passes personally, but I could have left them at will call. I should have. In fact, I should go do that now. I could turn in my own ticket and it'd probably get snapped up by someone who came hoping for a no-show. Then I could go home and put on some mindless television or read a book or something—anything—that would keep me from having to try to have a conversation with Preston now that he knew my secret. The secret I couldn't afford to have get out into common Gilead knowledge.

I turned and had taken half a step, when I caught a glimpse of him. Not that it had to be Preston, of course. Except that I knew it was, the same way I knew I was breathing in and out. Without thought. He was like a magnet to a piece of my soul.

I didn't like it.

"Wendy!" Preston raised a hand and the two men beside him turned.

I wanted to fan my face and possibly swoon. If it had been the 1800s, I absolutely would have gone with it. It didn't seem right for one family to produce three men who looked like that. Well, more than three. I'd seen posters of the twins who made up *Further Up and In*. Their talent wasn't the only reason they were a popular group.

Preston closed the distance between us. He gestured to his right. "This is my brother Cooper. And this"—he gestured to his left—"is Grayson."

"Pleasure to meet you." I reached out and shook Cooper's hand, then turned to do the same for Grayson. "Wait. Do you write sci-fi?"

He lit up. "I do."

"I've read a couple of your books. They're great." I shook his hand a little more forcefully. They'd been an impulse buy during one of my many insomnia-filled nights when nothing seemed to be able to catch or hold my attention. His books had. "I can't wait to find out what happens next on Vastarn."

"Yeah? That's awesome." Grayson looked at Preston. "Did you hear that? She's read my books."

Preston nodded. "I did."

"Sorry, I guess I could have asked. But honestly, Swift isn't exactly the most uncommon name in the world. What are the chances?" I hunched my shoulders a little.

"It's fine." Preston turned slightly and nudged Grayson in the side. "She recognized the twins though."

Cooper snorted out a laugh.

Grayson groaned. "Of course she did."

I winced. "Really only because they've been a topic at staff meetings for more than a year."

"Are they going to come at the end of the term?" Preston's full attention was on me and it did strange things to my insides.

I swallowed. "Yeah. Last I heard they were going to be on campus for chapel and an evening concert. I appreciate you putting in a word."

"I really didn't do anything more than mention that GG went here." Preston shrugged it away before looking at his watch. "I should probably get into the concession area. Letty doesn't like it if we're late."

I chuckled. I had a hard time seeing Letty as some kind of whip-cracking taskmaster, but maybe she took the concessions more seriously than I knew. Or Preston was teasing. Also possible. Probable, even. And I didn't know what to make of it.

He knew all my dirty laundry. All the things I worked hard to keep hidden from the community here in Gilead. Just because the situation with Letty's secret being revealed had worked out well with the town coming together to support her didn't mean they'd do the same for me.

I reached into my pocket and withdrew three lanyards. "These will get you in backstage. I made sure the manager knows to expect the three of you, and Mr. Miles is looking forward to saying hello."

Grayson reached out to take the passes. "Seriously? This is awesome. Thanks."

"You're welcome." I hadn't really done more than make a couple of phone calls. I cleared my throat. "I guess I'll let you all get settled. Enjoy the show."

"You're not staying?" Preston frowned. "I could have come to pick these up. I didn't think—"

"It's not a problem. I was happy to bring them over." I glanced at Preston's brothers. "You're awfully early. They won't open the doors for at least another thirty minutes."

"It's not a problem. We'll just find a wall and sit." Cooper tucked his hands in his pockets. "Preston explained that he'd be working."

I bit my lip. "There's a petting zoo out front and some other entertainment, if you wanted."

Preston chuckled. "I offered that. The consensus seems to be that petting zoos are for kids."

That was a fair point. And it was definitely the more obvious clientele. "Do you want me to stay? I'd be happy to."

"I'm not going to say no. You can fill me and Gray in on how Preston's been behaving." Cooper's eyes glittered with humor.

Preston shook his head. "I don't know why you'd volunteer to babysit these two, but it's your choice. I really appreciate the backstage passes. I'll see you later?"

I nodded, purely because his last words had sounded like a question. Of course I'd see him later. He was living here and Gilead was a small town. Not that I hadn't found ways to avoid him before, but I wasn't going out of my way to do that now. We'd made peace. And it seemed like the best way to be sure he kept my secret was to stay on his good side. "Actually, could I talk to you for a second?"

Preston's eyebrows lifted, but he stepped aside.

I took a few more steps away from his brothers and spoke in a low voice. "I just wanted to be sure you understand the things I told you...I really would appreciate you keeping them to yourself."

"Of course. I would never—" He broke off and disappointment coated his features. "You really think so little of me?"

"No. I just—I haven't—no one has known for so long, it's hard for me to accept that now someone does. But I wouldn't have said anything if I didn't trust you." The words were out before I realized I was going to say them. I was even more surprised by the fact that I meant them. I rested my hand on his arm and held his gaze. "I trust you."

His lips quirked up and he nodded. "Okay. Your secret is safe with me." He paused. "*You* are safe with me."

I looked away, unable to figure out how to process that. "You should go. We don't want Letty sending out a search party."

"Right. Thanks for babysitting my brothers." Preston shot me a thoughtful look before waving at his brothers and striding off toward the concessions.

I walked back to where Preston's brothers had their heads together, whispering. Sitting on the floor waiting for the doors to open didn't hold a lot of excitement to me. Thankfully, I worked at the college. "There's an office down this way that should be empty. It's got chairs that are more comfortable than the floor. Sound good?"

Grayson grinned. "Absolutely."

The two men fell into step with me, one on either side. "I always wondered what it'd be like to have brothers."

"Noisy." Cooper glanced at Grayson. "And mostly annoying."

"Oh yeah, cause you're a daydream to be around." He rolled his eyes before looking at me. "You don't have siblings?"

"One sister. Younger by enough years that as we got older, our relationship suffered." Since the accident, Whitney and I were mending things. More than that, we'd been forging more of a relationship than we'd really ever had. But it was hard. And I was probably to blame. I wasn't the poster child of openness. And Whitney was busy with her own life.

"I get that. The twins are five years behind me. There were a lot of times as a teenager that I didn't want anything to do with babies who were still in elementary school." Cooper laughed. "Now? I'm so proud of them I could burst. They're really coming here?"

"They are. I'm grateful your brother arranged it. I imagine he did more than he's letting on."

"Nah. We all love GG. Once Walker and Dawson made that

connection? It was a done deal. They would've bumped an existing date to make it happen if it would make GG happy." Grayson glanced at Cooper, as if for approval. "We all would. In some ways, all six of us are mama's boys. And Grandmother's boys. And GG's boys."

"We have some strong women in our family and we love them dearly. That's what Gray's trying to say in his weird, round-about way." Cooper shook his head. "Writers, right?"

I laughed and paused at a door that had a number pad above the handle. "Let's hope they haven't changed the code."

I punched in the numbers that I was reasonably sure would get us in, and held my breath. The door clicked and the handle unlocked. "Phew."

Cooper chuckled. "The floor would've been fine if it didn't work."

"Speak for yourself." I pushed open the door and gestured for the guys to go in.

The lights were on a motion sensor, so the space brightened almost immediately, revealing a couch along one wall, a desk with neatly stacked papers covering most of the surface, and three chairs.

"Have a seat." I opted for one of the chairs. It wasn't the most comfortable, but I didn't want to end up on the couch with one of Preston's brothers. The two of them sat next to one another on the sofa. I focused on Grayson. "You're not going to kill off Leta, right?"

Grayson's eyebrows lifted and he squirmed slightly in his seat. "Um."

"No way. You absolutely can't." Leta was a side character, it was true, but she was the sole reason I kept reading. I studied him. "You're trying to fool me."

Cooper nudged Grayson in the side. "I don't think she's buying your bluff."

"Had to try." Grayson flashed a grin. "Of course not. I'm thinking of spinning her off into her own series. She's great, right?"

I nodded.

We passed the next twenty minutes talking about Grayson's books. Cooper obviously was a fan as well—whether because he was a supportive brother or because he actually liked sci-fi, I couldn't quite figure out—but he knew the books.

The noise of the crowd out in the theater foyer gradually penetrated the quiet of the office where we sat. I checked the time.

"Oh. I should let you get to your seats. You don't want to miss the start." And then I'd go to my own seat. I doubted I was anywhere near them, having barely managed to squeak a seat when I finally decided to sit in the audience again tonight. "It's been fun getting to know you two. Your family is special."

Cooper laughed. "It sounds like you actually mean that in a positive way. Not in the way where people put quotation marks around it to indicate that we're a little off."

"Absolutely a positive way." I smiled. "I'm glad you came to visit your brother and see the play."

"As much as I think the play will be fun, I'm more looking forward to flying to Virginia tomorrow to meet Preston's new friend. Scott, I think he said?" Grayson looked at Cooper for confirmation.

"Yeah. Scott Wright. Wait. He's your brother-in-law, right?" Cooper looked at me.

I nodded, numb. Preston was leaving? Not that he had to clear his schedule with me. I wasn't his keeper. Or his mother. Or his girlfriend.

But I'd thought I was at least his girl friend. A friend who was a girl. Woman. Whatever.

Why hadn't he mentioned that he was leaving?

I missed a lot of what the two of them said as I held the door for them, a smile frozen on my face.

Preston was leaving.

He'd come back. Obviously. Because he had concessions duty on the weekend. And it wasn't as if we saw each other all the time during the week. In fact, we barely saw each other at all unless one of us made an effort to make it happen.

I managed to keep up light and breezy conversation as I helped them find the right door to go in to get to their seats. Then I made my way to the other side of the auditorium where my own seat waited.

Why hadn't he mentioned it?

Because I didn't matter.

And that was fine. Good, even.

I smiled absently at the usher as I showed her my ticket and made my way to the correct aisle and then slid past the already seated patrons to my empty seat.

I nodded once to myself as I settled in. So what? He and his brothers would fly to Virginia and hang out with Scott and Whitney. I had no right to feel blindsided by it.

Preston Swift didn't owe me anything.

18

PRESTON

I kicked my shoes off inside the door to my little on campus apartment, dropped my bag, and sighed. It was good to be home. Or what approximated as home for now, at least. For the next four weeks. I was ready to go home to Chicago. Even with the ridiculous décor in my place there. And honestly? I was going to change it. I had the money, and it was time for me to live in a place that matched my style. If Grandmother had an issue with it? Well, we'd talk it out. But the reality was that she'd made it my home. It was time to make it an actual home, not a resting place.

Or I'd find another place to live.

I didn't think that would go over well with Mom or Grandmother. So I was reasonably sure they'd both be fine with me getting rid of the magazine interior design and replacing it with something that worked for me.

Funny how seeing the livable—homey, even—place that Scott and Whitney called home had made that clear to me.

I'd enjoyed a lot about my trip to Virginia with Coop and Gray. Scott Wright had a great group of friends there in Old

Town Alexandria. And their story of making billions—literally —in the stock market was beyond. Good for them, though.

Even better? All of that group seemed committed to using their money to glorify God. The same thing our family had always emphasized. We were incredibly blessed. Sure, it was business. And sure, we had to make smart choices and smart decisions. But at the same time, everything we had came from God and we owed it to Him to steward it wisely.

I prayed for wisdom at the start of every work day. Running the family company might have been something I was raised to do, but I took the responsibility seriously. I owed it to every employee we had—every customer we had—to run things in a way that honored God and used His resources in the best possible way.

It had also been interesting to get to know Wendy's sister, Whitney, a little bit. They were very different people. Not that I was identical to any of my brothers, but we had more in common than it seemed like Wendy and Whitney did. And Whitney seemed unhappy about that. I was going to see if there was anything I could do to encourage Wendy to let her sister in.

I checked the time as I settled on the couch. GG had left a voicemail while I was on the plane. I hadn't wanted to have the distraction of driving when I called her back. But she ought to still be in her room. I tapped her contact and smiled as it rang.

"There's my favorite oldest grandson."

I laughed. "Good qualifications, GG. But I'm still going to rub it in to the others."

"I expect nothing less. How was your trip to Virginia?"

I shook my head. GG was still plugged into the family grapevine. I hadn't mentioned it to her—just to Mom. Of course, anything Mom knew, Grandmother was soon to find out. Apparently, that also trickled down to GG. "Good. It's nice to meet more people with money and similar values."

"That's good. It can be hard. Your great-grandfather always struggled to know who his real friends were. Even though we didn't have the same level of money then as the family does now, it was enough to be a challenge at times." GG coughed. "Excuse me."

"You sound a little better." Just a little. But I was glad that her cough seemed shorter and not as wet. "They're taking good care of you?"

"Don't worry about me, honey. I'm ready to be with Jesus and your great-granddad. But I'll stick around here as long as the Lord requires."

I frowned. As much as I appreciated her faith and the knowledge that our goodbye on Earth wouldn't be forever, I didn't like to hear her talk like that. I wanted my family—all of it—to stay the same. Losing GG was going to be a big event. "Well, selfishly, I hope that's a long time yet."

"When do you come back to Chicago? I miss our in-person visits."

"The play ends in four weeks, but I can fly up during the week." I should have thought of that. It would have been easy enough to get on the same flight as Cooper and Grayson and go visit GG before heading to Kansas. It wasn't as though I had some integral part in the play. I was just part of the concessions team. They'd manage without me on Friday night.

"No, that's fine. I was just wondering. I'll still be here."

"You better be." I sighed. "What if I came and got you for Easter services? I know you probably planned to just go to chapel there, but I also know everyone at church would love to see you. Then you could stay for the big meal Grandmother and Mom put together. We'll make it a day."

"I'd like that. Let me talk to the nurses and see if they think I'd be okay to do that."

"Why wouldn't you be?" I drummed my fingers on my leg. "Is there something going on with you that I don't know?"

"I'm sure it's nothing. This cough is just lingering longer than they like."

That's pretty much what they'd told me when I followed up after our last call. And she did sound like she'd improved since then. But also? "I'm not going to spring you if it's going to set you back. Why don't you let me check with them about our plan?"

"You don't trust me?"

I grinned at the suspicion in her voice. "I trust you, GG. I also love you and don't want to be the reason I lose you."

"Oh, Preston." Her words came out as a sigh. "You know I'm not going to live forever. You need a woman in your life."

My eyebrows lifted. "I do?"

"I try not to push. I know it's not popular to get married at nineteen anymore, but honey, you're halfway through your thirties. Don't you think it's time?"

"GG. You need to take that up with God. I'm not exactly beating them off with sticks." And it wasn't like I could go the usual route of dating apps. Maybe there was one for billionaires that I didn't know about—but all the normal ones had too many possibilities of finding someone who just wanted the money. Or a hookup. Or both. And I didn't want either of those things.

"Have *you* taken it up with God?"

I groaned. "Not recently. Ish."

"What does that mean?" She perked up. "Are things developing with a certain someone in Kansas?"

"I don't know. Maybe? Except it's complicated. She's had a complicated life. And, honestly, her whole life is here. I don't know that she'd be willing to move. And I need to be in Chicago. Living in Gilead isn't a long-term possibility. Cooper's been trying to keep things going, but his heart's not in it."

"No. Cooper needs to figure out his calling still. I hoped

maybe some time in charge with you too far away to step in would help him see Swift as a viable option."

"I did, too, GG. But he's more miserable than I've seen him in a while." I rubbed my forehead. Cooper was going to have to figure it out for himself, though. I could—and would—help however possible. It still needed to be him deciding what that calling was. "So. I need to be in Chicago and Wendy seems to belong here."

"Seems to?"

She *would* catch that. "I haven't talked to her about it. I thought things were moving in a direction where I would have. Then she pretty clearly showed me that I was misreading things. And now I don't know what's happening between us. Maybe nothing. Maybe friendship. Like I said, it's complicated."

"All the good things are. I'll pray for you. And for her." GG paused and I fully expected her to ask for more information, but she didn't.

"I'm going to let you go, GG. I love you."

"Love you, too, Preston. And I'm proud of you. Remember that."

"I will. And I'll call the front to see about springing you for Easter when I'm home, okay?"

"Okay. Bye now."

The phone went quiet, confirming my suspicion that she was more tired than she wanted to let on. I would definitely follow up with the staff there—not just because I'd like to have her at home for Easter. But I'd also explore my other information sources.

I tapped out a quick text to Mom. If there was something to know, Mom probably knew it. Or she'd find out.

With that done, I tried to focus on work, but my mind kept wandering to Wendy. After a couple hours of getting very little done, I stood, grabbed my phone, put my shoes back on, and headed out for a walk.

If my path happened to take me past the administration building, it wasn't like there were lots of options to choose from.

That wasn't entirely true, but I could roll with it for now.

It was warmer now that it was March, but the wind was still present. The farmland that surrounded Gilead was probably going to start bustling before much longer. I didn't know a lot about the rhythms of farms, for all that Swift was part of the food industry. We dealt more with cattle—that was what happened when you started out based in Chicago—and even then, we didn't have our own animals. We worked with ranchers to provide the already-slaughtered beef, and then we took it from there.

Of course, we didn't just deal with meat these days. Or even only food. Expansion was a necessary part of a company like ours. But our core would always be in beef. Still, was there some way for us to work with the farmers out here? It was something to ponder. GG would, I was sure, be for anything that helped keep Gilead, Kansas, on the map. And now, having spent a couple of months here, I could understand that a little better.

"Out for a walk?"

I stopped and turned at Wendy's voice. How had I missed her? I nodded. "Needed to stretch my legs. And my focus was off."

She laughed. "I'm having the same problem with focus. Happens every year as the weather starts warming up and the sun is out. It's probably too early to call it spring fever, but there you have it."

"Can you join me?" I hadn't intended to offer. I'd told GG the truth—I had no idea what Wendy and I were these days. I wasn't even positive friendship was something I could claim with complete honesty. I was attracted to her, no question, but that wasn't going to be a foundation for a long-lasting marriage.

"Yeah, okay." Wendy tucked her hands in the pockets of her coat as she fell into step beside me. "Have a good visit in Virginia?"

I took a moment to analyze her tone before answering. "I did. Are you mad at me?"

"No." She scowled down at the sidewalk for a few steps. "Maybe a little. You didn't tell me you were leaving town."

"Oh." I knew better than to say I hadn't thought of it, even if that was the truth. But why had she wanted to be kept in the loop? Was it general curiosity, or something more? "I'm sorry."

"It's fine. I'm not your mother. Or your keeper. I guess I just figured going out to visit my sister and brother-in-law would be something you mentioned to me." Wendy shrugged, like it was no big deal, but her face said otherwise.

I stopped and stepped in front of her then waited until she met my gaze. "I'm really sorry. I didn't think about it from that direction."

Wendy looked away. "I shouldn't be upset. It's stupid."

"No. You're allowed to feel how you feel. Can you tell me why though?"

"Why what?"

I shifted back to my position at her side and resumed walking. "Why are you upset?"

"Because everything is easy for Whitney." Her words spewed out in a rush.

My eyebrows lifted. That...wasn't anywhere close to something I expected. And I didn't have any idea how to respond. I hadn't actually spent much time with Whitney. I'd gone to get to know Scott and his guy friends more than anything. And while, yes, we'd hung out in a big group that included Whitney and several of her friends here and there, it wasn't like I had long conversations with her.

"Don't worry. I realize how that sounds." Wendy massaged the space between her eyebrows. "It's not even completely true. It just feels true a lot of the time."

"I'm sorry." That was safe, right?

"I'm being stupid. When your brothers mentioned you were flying out, I was frustrated. And I guess I didn't understand why you wouldn't mention it."

"Honestly? I didn't think you'd care."

She nodded—sort of an absent acknowledgment of my words more than anything. She sighed. "I did. Do. What's going on here, Preston?"

Wendy stopped and shaded her eyes as she looked at me.

I sorted through different ways to answer. But the truth was probably the best place to start. "I don't know."

19

WENDY

I hovered at the back of the worship center and scanned the crowd—such as it was. I was simultaneously trying to avoid my parents and also find Preston.

His words from our walk had echoed in my head all weekend. What had I expected from him? It was mortifying. I'd put him on the spot and he'd answered. I should be happy with that. I didn't know what was going on between us, either. So it wasn't as if I had some answer that he'd failed to find.

And yet that was exactly what I'd hoped for in the moment.

"Hey."

I turned and my breath caught as I met Preston's gaze. "Hi. I was hoping I'd see you. I wanted to apolo—"

"Please don't." He shook his head before turning to look at the filling seats. "Will you sit with me?"

"I...yeah. I'd like that." I swallowed, my mouth suddenly dry. Friends. My end goal here was for the two of us to be friends. Then, when he headed back to Chicago in four weeks, I'd have a friend in Chicago who maybe would touch base now and then and give me a glimpse of the larger world out there beyond the confines of Gilead.

We walked down the side aisle until we found a couple of empty seats. Preston let me go in ahead of him, which was nice but I would have preferred the aisle. Then again, with his long legs, maybe that was the same for him. Of the two of us, I was the one who wouldn't struggle with legroom in an inside seat.

"Do you want to maybe get lunch at the diner after church?" Preston glanced at me.

I tried to read his expression and failed. "Do you want to eat there, specifically, or do you just want to have lunch together?"

"I was angling for lunch. Why?"

"I'd rather fix something at home. The diner is fine. It's just... the diner." It was the place I ate all the time. The place Mark had insisted on every single Sunday after church. It was where so many memories of my girls lived—good and bad ones—and I didn't want to deal with their ghosts today. At least not more than I had to. It wasn't as if they ever went away. Not completely. But at home, the memories were quieter. More bearable. Maybe because I was there more?

His lips curved. "I'll never say no to something home cooked. I didn't want to impose."

"You're not."

Preston started to speak, but the worship team took the stage and called us to stand.

I made it through the service. I can't say I remembered a lot of what the pastor talked about, but that was fairly common these days. So much of me hurt already, it was like I couldn't listen too closely in case there was something convicting. Something that was going to rip off whatever tender scabs I might have.

It needed to change. I knew that. I just didn't know how to do it. All I could do—or at least, all I could think to do—was pray for Jesus to heal me. And He was. But it was slower than I would have liked.

I looked at Preston as the quiet strains of post-service music started. "Ready?"

"Yeah. I'll meet you there. Can I stop at the store and pick anything up?"

I shook my head.

"All right. See you in a few."

I gathered my purse, tucking my phone into the front pocket, and started down the aisle after Preston.

"Wendy."

I stopped and closed my eyes, breathing in and steadying myself, before I stepped out of the stream of people and waited for Mom to catch up. "Hi, Mom."

"I'm glad you made it. I looked for you and thought you might be skipping again today." Her gaze searched my face.

"I'm okay, Mom. I'm not going to go back there again." We never really discussed the bone-deep depression that had plagued me since the accident. I was better enough now, that I was functioning, and as far as my parents knew, I was back to fine. Other than the blip in the fall when they'd cut their Caribbean trip short because of me.

"You know we're here for you. Regardless of whether or not you do."

"I do. But I'm fine."

Mom shook her head. "You always say that. I don't know how to believe it anymore. But I'm trying to take your word for it."

"Would it help you to know I invited Preston to lunch?" I didn't really want to tell her that. She was going to make more out of it than there was, but maybe it would also soothe some of her fears. I had always loved to cook. And entertain. This was a tiny step back to that part of myself that I'd lost along with my family.

"It doesn't hurt." Mom winked. "I won't invite myself over. Nor will I remind you of just how handsome he is."

"Mom."

She held up her hands. "I'm not doing any of that. I'm just going to say that I'm praying that you'll let yourself dream a little again. You stopped doing that a long time before the accident. And now, maybe you're in a place where you can start again."

I frowned slightly, my eyebrows drawing together. "I don't know what you mean."

Mom sighed and patted my cheek. "You were never like Whitney. She'd tell everyone in her life everything about her life at the slightest encouragement. But I always thought I was pretty good at reading my girls. And maybe it's time for me to remind you that I'm always here for you. I always have been. And you never have to go through things alone."

I couldn't find the right words. She couldn't possibly know about Mark. Could she? The girls...would they have mentioned things to their Nana? They'd known better, surely. If Mark had found out...it didn't bear consideration.

Mom had already walked back to join Dad. I watched as he slipped his arm around her shoulders and the two of them exited in the other direction.

All my life, I'd wanted a marriage like my parents had. Mark had put on a pretty good show at the beginning. And there'd been so many promises. He'd do better. He was sorry. I was sorry. I'd change so I didn't irritate him after a long day. I'd spent years striving to be perfect, when perfection was never something I was going to attain.

I sighed and headed out toward the parking lot, managing to smile and exchange greetings with anyone who approached. I was good at faking normal.

I was good at faking a lot of things.

Maybe it was time for that to change.

I got in my car and headed home. When I arrived, Preston had already parked on one side of the driveway. He got out as I pulled in beside him and shut off the engine. I checked that I had everything before opening the door and getting out.

"I was beginning to wonder if I misunderstood." He grinned and his tone was light. Teasing.

"Sorry. Mom caught me." I shook my head.

"Is my being here causing problems?"

"No." I started toward the front door. "But she's probably going to start measuring you for a tux. Fair warning."

"As long as it's not to *bury* me in, I think I'll be okay." Preston followed me through the front door and closed it behind himself. "Can we talk about the other night?"

I hooked my purse on the doorknob of the coat closet and stepped out of my shoes. I looked at him over my shoulder. He was toeing his shoes off on the mat inside the door. "If you feel like we need to. I put you on the spot. It was unfair to ask you something I didn't know myself."

"That's the thing." Preston followed me into the kitchen and took a seat on a stool at the counter while I went to the sink to wash my hands. "I don't know what's going on here, but I'd like to figure it out. I guess at this point, I feel like I know you well enough to put my cards on the table."

I raised my eyebrows even as my stomach clenched. I turned to the fridge and opened the door, trying to keep my hands busy so my nerves wouldn't show. "Okay."

Preston waited while I gathered an armful of ingredients and set them on the counter.

I cleared my throat. "I didn't ask. Is steak salad all right? I can make something more manly, if you'd rather. I have steak, obviously, I could do rice and peas instead."

"Salad's great. The meals in the dining hall are always a little heavier than I'm used to. I've started just going for one meal. I don't have the will power to make good choices when there are so many other options available that I don't have to cook."

His easy grin eased some of my tension, while setting off a whole separate set of feelings that I didn't want to study too closely. Not right now, at least, while he was sitting in my kitchen. I offered a brief smile before turning on the grill that was built into my stovetop to get it heating.

"So. Cards." Preston drummed out a rapid tattoo on the counter. Maybe he was nervous, too? "I'm interested in seeing where a relationship with you could go. You're smart, funny, and beautiful and exactly the sort of woman I've imagined marrying most of my adult life. But I also realize there are some big hurdles. Your life is here, in Gilead, and as nice as it's been to hang out here the past couple of months, my life is in Chicago. I can't change that. And, to be honest, I don't really want to."

I looked up from seasoning the steaks, blood thundering in my ears. I worked to keep my face from reflecting the tidal wave of conflicting emotions that washed over me. In reality, we barely knew each other. He hadn't been in Kansas long. And while we'd had conversations about Mark and the girls and all of that, the fact remained that I'd only known him since January. And if a whirlwind courtship with Mark had taught me anything, it was that I needed to slow down and pay more atten- tion to God when it came to things like this.

I kept my voice as casual as I could when I answered, "I don't blame you. There's no comparison between Chicago and Kansas."

"Which I guess, leads me to my first question: is there any way you'd ever consider leaving here?"

"Only in a heartbeat." I carefully laid the steaks on the grill, smiling slightly at the hissing sizzle that accompanied the action.

"Really? But your parents and the college?" Preston straight- ened. "I just figured..."

"My parents would travel more if they weren't worried about

me. They're still healthy and active and right now, don't need me here. There's a big part of me that suspects they'd move to DC or maybe Florida if they knew, for certain, that I'd be okay without them so close by." I opened the container of pre-washed mixed greens and got down two plates. "I guess what I'm saying is that you shouldn't—I shouldn't—let Gilead be the thing in the way."

"Okay. That's really great." He rubbed his hands on his legs. "My second question, and I think I know the answer but I figure I should ask, is if my family money bothers you."

I laughed. "Seriously?"

He shrugged. "You'd be surprised. The women who aren't actively interested in me *because* of my money often find it a problem. There are news articles and cameras and, while it hasn't been an issue in Kansas really, in Chicago it happens more often. And I tend to avoid a lot of public outings because of it."

Hm. Scott and his friends had mostly avoided the public eye, although there'd been a big issue last spring that caused Austin to quit working as a high school math teacher. In the end, it had all worked out for the best, but at the time it had been awful. For all of them. Now things had settled, from what I understood. "I've never minded being a homebody."

I flipped the steaks over and pressed each one lightly with my finger. They were getting there. I carried tomatoes and a bell pepper to the sink to wash them before I cubed them for the salads.

"What would you want to do?"

I glanced up at him. "What do you mean?"

"For a job. Would you want one? Or, I mean, I wouldn't mind starting a family. But that doesn't mean you couldn't work." He stopped and ran a hand through his hair. "Maybe I'm getting ahead of myself."

"No. No, it's fine. It's maybe a little unusual, since we aren't even officially dating yet. But these are all conversations that need to happen. More than once. And in more detail than we're getting to here, if I'm honest."

Mark and I had skipped—or skimmed—a lot of these talks. Both of us had gone into things high on physical tingles and swoony romance. Or I had. Mark had, apparently, been more calculated about the whole thing. Either way, he'd had his assumptions and I'd had mine, and I hadn't done anything about it when I'd started to realize the issues before we married. Because it would have been too embarrassing. The invitations had been sent. Gifts received. Mom and Dad would have supported me calling it off. They would have been confused, certainly, but they would have been on my side.

"I'm not opposed to having more children. I had easy preg-nancies. I'll admit the idea is a little scary, but my therapist would love for me to talk it through with her." I managed a wan smile. "I come with a lot of baggage. I'm pretty sure you could find someone easier to be with in about six seconds."

"That might be true, but I don't want to. I want to give things a try. With you."

I swallowed and studied his face. He looked so earnest. I was terrified. But also intrigued. And...hopeful? I took a deep breath. "I'd like that, too."

20

PRESTON

I couldn't have stopped the grin if I'd wanted to. And I definitely did not want to. It didn't guarantee anything. The hurdles we were looking at were definitely something that we'd have to work on. But we'd be doing it together.

"Cool."

She laughed and took the steaks off the grill. "Cool? Really?"

"Apparently." I breathed in and my mouth watered. "Is there anything I can do to help?"

"Now that I'm almost finished? Good timing." Her grin belied any hint of censure in her tone. "You could fix us some tea. There should be a pitcher in the fridge. I'm assuming you remember where the glasses are?"

"Sure." I slid off the stool and made my way to the cabinet that held the drinking glasses, then carried two over to the fridge to fill. "Do you think you'd have any time to fly to Chicago with me? I know my GG would like to meet you. Mom and Grandmother, too, for that matter."

"Um." She glanced over her shoulder at me and set the knife she was holding down on the counter. "That seems fast."

"Does it? I know they wouldn't agree, but I've mentioned you in too many conversations for them not to wonder."

"You've mentioned me?" Wendy picked up the knife again and began slicing the steaks into neat strips. When she finished, she slid the knife under and transferred the meat to the top of the salad.

I cleared my throat. "It started out just working with you for the endowment and such, but then...yes. I mentioned you. All the while, assuring them that nothing was going to come of it. So you have that going for you."

"Oh, man. They're not even going to like me, are they?"

"Coop and Gray did. That's a big boost in your favor. And GG does. Mom and Grandmother are probably going to be more reserved, but they just want me to be happy." I put the glasses of tea down on the counter and crossed to where she stood. I hesitated a moment before opening my arms and lifting an eyebrow in invitation.

Wendy looked at me and my heart thundered in my chest. She slowly set the knife down and wiped her hands on the kitchen towel that she'd flung over her shoulder earlier. Then, finally, she stepped into my arms.

I tightened my grasp and closed my eyes as I laid my cheek on the top of her head. I was a fan of hugs—always had been— but this had to be the best hug I'd ever experienced. And that was saying something, because we had some good huggers in my family. I smiled, amused at myself. "I didn't mean tomorrow. Just soon. Okay?"

"Okay. Maybe after Easter?"

When I was already back in Chicago. That made more sense, probably, than both of us traveling from Gilead for a day or two. I didn't really want to wait, but if I knew anything about life, it was that waiting was part of it. Frequently. "Sure. That's a good idea."

Wendy's arms contracted in a squeeze before she eased back.

"Ready to eat?"

"Definitely. It smells amazing." I got the glasses from the counter and followed Wendy as she carried the two plates into the dining room. She set them down, one at the head of the table, the other on the right of that chair. I was glad we could sit next to one another, instead of across from as we had previously.

I put the glasses down and reached for the back of the chair to pull it out, then hesitated. "Can I get your chair for you?"

"Thank you." She waited as I pulled out the chair, then she sat and I gave the seat a little push as she scooted in. "Do I need to apologize again?"

"No. I want you to be comfortable though. We can figure out a way that we're both happy. Right?"

She nodded. "I don't really mind your manners. I was having a bad day that day. I really am sorry."

"Okay. But tell me, please. I don't want to do something that's hurtful to you." I reached out, palm up. "Can I pray for the food?"

She put her hand in mine. It was warm, and soft. And right. I gave it a quick squeeze before closing my eyes to bless the food.

Lunch conversation flowed easily to other, less serious topics. I told her about the trip to Virginia in more detail—there were some amusing stories about her nephew to share—and the things I missed about Chicago.

When the plates were cleared and the kitchen tidied, we settled on the couch in the family room. I looked around. It was homey. Her whole house was. It was welcoming and warm and exactly the kind of space I would want to live in.

"Did you decorate everything yourself or hire someone?"

Her eyebrows lifted. "I did it. Mom helped. Mark…"

I waited a moment, but she didn't continue. I rubbed her leg. "I don't mind if you talk about him. Good things. Bad things. In-between things. He was part of your life."

She took a deep breath and blew it out. "Okay." She nodded and swallowed. "Okay. Mark wanted to hire someone. It was one of our first big fights. I won, obviously, but he never really let me forget it. Even though the business contacts we entertained all commented on how much they liked it."

I wanted to tell her how sorry I was, but I could sense that wasn't what she wanted. Or needed. "You did a good job. In fact, maybe you can help me redecorate my place when you come to Chicago."

"Sure, if you want."

Her response lacked enthusiasm. "Or not. I don't want you to feel like you have to work. I can find a designer in town and have them do it."

"It's not that. I'm just not sure I know how to decorate a Chicago apartment. This is Kansas, you know? It's not farm-house chic, but it's not far off. You don't want to live in that."

"I don't?" I looked around the room again. I'd be pretty happy with this as my family room. I'd be happy with any of the rooms in her house. "I like your house. Staying here in January was a highlight of that trip."

Wendy squirmed, then finally scooted to the side, putting a little distance between us. "How about this. I'll think about it and take a look when I come out to visit. If I get some ideas, we can talk about them and go from there."

That was reasonable. I didn't want her to be reasonable, though. I wanted her to be excited and planning a future with me, the way my mind had already started to do. Which, admit-tedly, was too much too fast. But now that we'd stopped dancing around it, I was ready to dive in head first.

I was realizing that would send Wendy running in the oppo-site direction.

So I would slow down. Or at least keep my thoughts to myself.

"That sounds good. I can email you a link to some photos if you want to look at it again in more detail before then. No pressure, obviously. But it occurs to me you don't know much about where I live."

"Just Chicago. Well, that's not completely true. I did map your address. Are the views of the lake as amazing as it seems like they would be?"

I reached out to take her hand. "They absolutely are."

I PARKED in front of Heavenly Brew and climbed out of my car. I'd been grinning non-stop since Sunday afternoon. Coworkers had commented on it during some of our video chats. I didn't explain. One of the benefits of being in charge was that I could be happy without having to let everyone else in on why.

Wendy and I had started having lunch together in her office as well. Now that the busybody out front was gone because of her mishandling of the business with Letty's mom, it was a lot nicer to stop by the admin building. And today we were stretching our time together by adding in an afternoon coffee break. I didn't mind reshuffling my Wednesday to do it, but I'd been a tiny bit surprised when she'd asked at lunch.

She pulled up behind me and parked, then hopped out. "Hi. Were you waiting long?"

"No. Just got here." I reached out and took her hand as she approached. "This is a nice break."

"I'm glad. I just needed out of the office today. There's not a lot for me to do, and it's just..." She trailed off and gestured vaguely.

I chuckled. "I've had days like that."

I reached for the door to Heavenly Brew and held it for Wendy. The rich scent of coffee greeted me and my mouth watered. I didn't need caffeine this late in the day, but I wasn't going to complain. In fact, I might just get a pastry and call it dinner.

"Hi. What can I get you?" Letty beamed over the register at us.

"I'll have a caramel latte." Wendy glanced over her shoulder at me.

I stopped scanning the menu. "Can I do the same, but decaf?"

Letty wrinkled her nose, but rang up the order. "For here?"

"Yes. Can I get a turnover, too?" I pointed to the pastries in the case.

Letty added that in and told me the total. I pulled out money and, when Letty handed me change, dropped it in the tip jar.

Wendy tugged my hand. "Let's sit over in the corner."

I followed her to the table tucked a little bit away from the rest of the seating. "Won't you be up all night if you have a latte now?"

"I'm up most nights anyway, so that wouldn't be unusual. I don't find caffeine matters one way or the other."

I frowned slightly.

"Don't worry about it. Please." She squeezed my hand. "It's getting better. A lot better, recently."

"Okay." It was the right thing to say, but I was still going to worry. And more than that, I'd be sure to pray for Wendy at bedtime.

Letty called out that our order was ready. I stood. "Be right back."

At the counter, I set the plate with the turnover on top of the mug that Letty said held the decaf. The scent of sugar wafted around me as I carried the drinks to the table.

Wendy picked up her mug and took a sip. Her eyes closed. "Mmm."

I sniffed my coffee before following suit. It was definitely caramel. And so, so sweet. Not something I'd normally order. Nor something I would get again. But I could probably handle finishing one. I reached for my turnover and took a bite. "Have you looked at your calendar at all to see when you can come to Chicago?"

"Not yet. I need to do that. And check flights, all of that."

I tipped my head to the side. "I'll fly down and get you. I just need to know when."

"Oh. I…"

"What?"

"I've never flown like that. It's—I don't mind commercial."

"You're scared." I took a bite of turnover and nodded. "Understandable. And yet, I'm a very good pilot. You'll be safer with me—and more comfortable—than on a commercial flight." I smiled over the rim of my mug. "And I'd really like to show you what it's like."

Wendy looked down into her mug before taking a drink. "What if…"

While I waited, I took another bite of pastry and washed it down with a big sip of latte. She still hadn't spoken, so I did. "What if what? You already know better than most people how life can change in the blink of an eye. Trust me?"

It took a moment, but she nodded. "All right. If you're sure you have time."

"I'm sure." Cooper could fill in if she chose a date that was busy, but the reality was that with enough advance notice, I could make just about anything work.

Her grin flashed. "Mom wants you to come to dinner again."

"Okay. When?"

"Just like that?" She shook her head. "You realize now that we're dating it's not going to be the same as the last meal."

"I kind of doubt that, actually. Your parents seem like normal people who love and trust their daughter to make good deci-sions. Besides which, your dad already told me neither of them would mind if I could find a way to get you to go out with me."

Wendy blinked. "He did what?"

"A couple of Sundays ago, when I happened to think the chance of it happening was ridiculously small. Like microscopi-cally small. I told him that. He said he'd been praying about it and that I shouldn't give up hope. You just had to figure it out for yourself first." I took the last bite of pastry and brushed crumbs off the front of my shirt. "Turns out, he was right."

She shook her head. "That man."

"I like him."

She laughed. "You would."

"Like you don't."

"Eh. He's okay, as dads go, I guess."

"So. When's dinner?"

"Not sure. I'm supposed to have you check your calendar and give me dates."

"Oh yes, my bustling calendar. Other than play nights, I'm open. Tomorrow?" Mrs. Hall was a wonderful cook. Just like her daughter. I wasn't worried about showing up and finding myself on the menu, either. Mr. Hall had already made it clear they felt God had brought me to Gilead to help Wendy reengage in life.

I was happy to be part of that process.

I'd be content to continue being part of that process for as long as God allowed.

"I'll double-check with Mom, but it's probably good." She cocked her head to the side. "What are you thinking?"

It was too soon to tell her any of the things I was actually thinking, so I settled on something close enough to the full truth. "I like being with you."

The smile she gave did nothing to help me focus on taking things slowly.

"Wendy Hall." I answered the phone without looking away from my computer. The college board had emailed all the employees with the outline of a new fundraising campaign they were hoping to implement as part of the new school year in August.

I hadn't been aware the board was discussing new campaigns. Or that they were concerned that our current fundraising efforts weren't satisfactory. The whole email came as a shock and I'd now read it over three times trying to make sense of it.

We didn't need a new building. Our expenses stayed a healthy amount under the budget each year. So why? Why were they drafting this huge capital campaign?

And why hadn't I been included?

I'd had no heads-up. No invitations to any meetings. I was just informed at the same time as the rest of the staff? It made me uneasy.

"Wendy, it's Darlene from church. Karen activated the prayer chain and your name is under mine. Wren, Zoey Matthews's daughter, fell in the fishing pond out at the truck farm."

Thoughts of the capital campaign fled. "The pond? It has to be freezing still."

"Yeah. She's on the way to the emergency room. Or already there by now most likely. But we need to pray."

I nodded even though Darlene couldn't see. "Of course. I'll do that right now. Can you remind me who I'm supposed to contact?"

"Your mom, hon."

"Well, that's easy." Except it wasn't. Not when a child's life hung in the balance. I breathed in through my nose and spent every ounce of effort I could on maintaining my calm. "I'll call her now. Thanks, Darlene."

"You bet. Bye."

I stared at the phone in my hand. Swallowing back the lump forming in my throat, I pressed the switch to get a dial tone and quickly punched in Mom's number.

It rang twice before she answered. "Hi, honey."

"Mom. Darlene called with the church prayer chain. I thought they'd switched to an email blast."

Mom chuckled. "They tried that, yes, but a lot of the older generation felt it took too long to know about prayer needs. They're not attached to a cell phone like so many are, and only check their email one or two times a day."

"Oh." I guessed that made sense. Although, it still felt like they could do both. Or a text alert. Something that wasn't reminiscent of the time when phones were newfangled technology.

"What's the prayer request?"

Right. I cleared my throat. "Zoey Matthews's daughter Wren fell in the fishing pond out at the truck farm. She's in emergency."

"Oh my. Are you all right?"

Trust Mom to understand and ask. The right answer—the true one—was no. But I didn't want to make this about me. "I'm okay. You should get on to the next name on the list. And then pray."

"I will. And then I'm calling you right back."

"No, Mom. I'm fine. I'm sure you're busy with whatever Tuesdays hold in your world." I should know. Mom had a pretty solid schedule. "I have work. Love you."

"Wendy—"

I hung up the phone and covered my face with my hands. A sob tore out of my throat. It was like every nerve ending was on fire. My memory flashed to the accident. Mark, not watching where he was going because he was too busy screaming at me. The girls, hunched up small in the back seat, crying soundlessly like they always did when Mark got like that. Then the impact— an explosion of pain that took my breath—and the screams in the backseat before darkness.

I took a shuddering breath and held it as long as I could. It helped. Sort of. Enough, at least, that I could quickly power down my computer, grab my cellphone and purse, and stand. I stared blankly around my office. I should...what?

Think, Wendy. Think.

I swallowed as nausea roiled in my stomach. I managed a mental wail at God. It would have to suffice as a prayer for Wren. I didn't have any words. I unlocked my phone and shot a quick text off to the only people who might come looking for me to let them know I wasn't feeling well and was going to take the rest of the day.

Then I hurried to my car.

Thankfully, they hadn't replaced the receptionist yet. Everyone else was busy working. So I didn't run into anyone and have to explain why tears were dripping down my cheeks. I didn't think I'd get a word out if I tried.

A small, rational part of my brain tried to remind me that this was different. Wren wasn't mine. And falling in the pond, while potentially serious, was unlikely to be fatal. Especially since she was already at the emergency room, which meant someone had noticed quickly and gotten her help. Temperatures had been in the midforties, at least, for the last week and a half, so while the water was absolutely cold, she'd probably be fine.

But it didn't matter. I couldn't bring up a picture of Wren in my mind, so I just saw my girls, cowering in the back of the car moments before it all changed. That was my last memory of them. That and their piercing shrieks.

I made it to my car and pulled the door handle. The car beeped cheerily as the doors unlocked. I climbed in, closed the door, and rested my head on the steering wheel. My hand flew to cover my mouth as a wail ripped free and I struggled to keep it together. I couldn't break down here.

I needed to go...where?

Home was out. Mom would come to the office. Then she'd go to my house. If my in-laws had possessed even an ounce of compassion, I'd have a place at the cemetery where I could go and sit. But they'd insisted that Mark and the girls be buried in the family plot in Mark's hometown. I'd been in a coma the whole time. Mom and Dad had tried, but no one won against Mark's parents once they'd made up their minds.

Preston?

Even as I discarded that idea, I started the engine. My hands shook on the wheel. It was probably a terrible idea to drive, but I needed to get away. To go...somewhere.

I tightened my grip and backed out of the parking spot. I could get on the highway and head toward Wichita. There was a marker on the side of the road. Maybe I could pull over and... what? Relive the accident?

I didn't need to be there for that. I just had to stop actively fighting the memories.

The passenger side front wheel bumped up and onto the curb, then back down as I turned out of the administration building parking lot. I stopped and held my shaking hands up, away from the wheel.

After three deep breaths, I tried again, easing into the lane that would take me around the campus perimeter.

My phone rang.

I ignored it, concentrating on driving. I should have turned it off. It was most likely Mom. Or Dad. Or the two of them together.

They'd want me to come to their house. Then they'd expect me to talk. But what was I supposed to say?

I turned the car into a parking lot and found a space before cutting the engine and blowing out a breath. I reached over and turned off my cell as it started to ring again. I should just go home.

But I didn't.

I pushed open the door and got out, automatically reaching for my purse, closing the door, and locking it.

I nodded to the students laughing in a little clump just outside the dorm as I hurried past them, head down, arms crossed tightly over my chest.

"Hey, Ms. Hall. How's it—"

I rushed past the RD at the desk without even glancing his direction. I banged my fist on Preston's door. Waited. Banged again.

I was getting ready for a third round, when Preston opened the door.

"Wendy. Hi. This is a surprise." He paused and stepped back. "Come in and you can tell me what's wrong."

I flung myself at him, letting go of the last shreds of control I'd had on my emotions. I vaguely registered him closing the door before his arms came around me. He rubbed little circles on my back as I sobbed incoherently into his shoulder.

I didn't know how long we stood there before he nudged me over to the couch. He sat, pulling me onto his lap, his strong arms never easing their comforting embrace as all the pent-up grief, anger, and confusion I harbored spilled out of me.

I don't remember falling asleep, but when I pried my eyes open and rubbed away the crusty remains of my tears, I was on the couch with a pillow under my head and a blanket covering me. Weak rays of sunlight crept through the windows, giving dim light that didn't hurt my head or eyes.

I cleared my throat and started to sit up.

"Can I get you some water? I could make tea?" Preston leaned forward in his chair and set his laptop on the coffee table.

"Water would be good." I cleared my throat again to try and erase the raspiness I'd heard in my voice. "Thank you."

"It's not a problem." He stood and disappeared in the direction of the kitchenette.

I swung my legs over the edge of the couch and straightened, then tugged the blanket back over my lap. I reached for the glass when he came back. "Thanks."

Preston sat on the edge of the coffee table, his knees bumping mine. "You're welcome. I think I got the gist of it from your mom when I called to let her know you were with me."

I winced and turned away.

"Do you want to talk about it?"

I shook my head, unable to meet his gaze.

Preston's hands closed over the fist I clenched in my lap. "Okay."

I sipped the water and looked at him. "That's it?"

He nodded. "Like I said, your mom filled me in as best as she could. I guess she thought this was overdue."

I scoffed. Maybe so. Didn't make it easier to hear. "I'm sorry."

"You don't need to apologize. I'm grateful you came to me. I would have worried." Preston's gaze was steady and devoid of censure.

Even still, guilt crept in. "Like my parents."

"They appreciated that I called. But they understand better than you give them credit for." He squeezed my hand. "Are you hungry at all? I happen to have a can of chicken noodle."

I opened my mouth to decline—to make excuses and hurry away. Instead, what came out was, "Okay."

He grinned, squeezed my hand again, and stood. Then, after a moment's hesitation, he leaned down and pressed a kiss to my forehead, before stepping away.

I turned, following his progress into the kitchenette. He moved with quiet competence as he got the familiar red and white labeled can from one of the cupboards, pulled the tab to open it, and dumped it into a saucepan he'd pulled out of a different cabinet. He added a can of water and stirred. Then looked back my way.

"What?"

I shook my head and raised the glass to my mouth. I didn't know how to put into words the vague disappointment that the first time he kissed me was a peck on my forehead. It had been sweet. Comforting, even.

But it just reinforced how incredibly broken I was.

"I don't think I can do this to you." I leaned forward and put the glass down on the coffee table.

"Do what, exactly?" Preston gave the soup another stir before looking my way.

"This. A relationship. I'm not a good bet, Preston. You have to realize that now. I thought I was doing better, but apparently that's a lie. I don't really even know Zoey Matthews or her daughter. There's no reason I should have responded that way."

"Wren's fine, by the way. Your mom said to be sure to tell you."

I looked down at my clasped hands. That was good. I would never wish for another mother to understand what it was to lose a child. And I hated that some small, dark part of me wished I'd had the chance to make Mark feel the pain of losing the girls. I wasn't convinced that I would've won in court, but I would have given it everything I had. There was a distinct possibility he didn't care enough about them—or me—to fight back. But now I'd never know. Because I'd lost them all instead.

"Wendy?"

I glanced up and over at Preston. "Yeah?"

"You're not doing anything to me. I'm here because I want to be. I'm with you because I want to be. The past two weeks since we agreed to see where this went have been exactly what I hoped they'd be."

"Until today."

Preston shook his head. "Nope. Including today. I love that you came to me. That you would trust me enough to come here."

"I didn't mean to." I covered my mouth. "I didn't mean to say that."

He chuckled. "It's okay."

It shouldn't be okay though. I was a mess. A big, broken mess who was finally realizing that I'd spent the bulk of my life trying to be perfect, because that was easier than getting rejected and hurt. Except it didn't stop either of those things from happening.

Preston got down bowls and poured soup into them. He opened and closed a few drawers before finding spoons and putting one in each bowl, then he carried them over to the coffee table.

"Here we are. One gourmet meal." He winked and tipped his head to the side. "Can I sit next to you?"

"Sure." I moved the edge of the blanket closer to my legs so he wouldn't have to sit on it. "Thank you."

"For what?"

"Everything."

He met my gaze and smiled. And for a moment, everything settled. All the jagged edges smoothed out. My chest didn't feel quite so tight.

I broke the contact and reached for my soup. I cradled it in my hands a moment, letting the warmth seep in, then scooped up a spoonful. The salty broth was just exactly right. "This is good."

Preston took a bite of his own soup. "Always hits the spot."

We sat in comfortable silence while we ate. He was close enough that the heat from his body warmed mine without touching. I contemplated sliding over and closing the space between us. I wanted that contact. The reassurance that he really didn't regret getting involved with me now that he'd seen what the reality was.

Preston brought his bowl to his mouth and tipped the last of the contents in, then leaned forward and set the empty bowl on the coffee table. As he moved back, he shifted closer so his leg touched mine from hip to ankle. He stretched his arm around the back of the couch behind me and curved his hand around my shoulder.

I didn't think, I just snuggled in.

"Want me to put on a movie?"

I felt the rumble of his voice from where my head rested on his shoulder. I nodded. "That sounds perfect."

22

PRESTON

I dragged my arm across my forehead as I stepped away from the fryers. The back area of the kitchen where the equipment was placed seemed to get particularly hot. I wandered toward the window, being careful to stay out of the way, although the crush had tapered off.

"Doing okay?"

I nodded at the girl—I'd forgotten her name. She was quiet and barely spoke so it wasn't hard. "I might take a little break. Peek in to the play for a minute."

The girl shrugged.

There were two others who were competent with the fryers at this point, so I wasn't going to worry about it. I just needed five minutes away from the heat and tedium of concessions. My family company might be food-oriented, but that didn't mean I wanted to be in the trenches with it.

I pushed through the door into the foyer and breathed deeply. It was cooler. And it didn't smell of the snacks mixing together into an aroma that bordered on unpleasant. I crossed to the nearest set of theater doors and eased one open just enough for me to slip through.

It took a second for my eyes to adjust to the darkness. I looked up to the well-lit stage. The actor playing Jesus was seated with a crowd around him. He had a child in his lap. I squinted—was it Wren? I'd done a little cyberstalking after the incident on Tuesday. Curiosity more than anything else, since I'd been attending the same church. I had, in fact, seen Zoey and Wren in the foyer. It was good to see the little girl fully recovered and seeming no worse for wear.

"I luff you, Mr. Connor." The girl slid off Jesus's lap and her words were just barely picked up by his mic. The audience chuckled, drowning out whatever he might have said in return.

I smiled. It was a sweet moment—even if he was supposed to be Jesus, not Mr. Connor. Had he been part of rescuing her? I hadn't gotten all the scoop on the accident, although it was absolutely the buzz in town. But I'd started sidestepping the conversations when it became clear that others were making connections between Wren's accident and Wendy's—and then they started fishing for how she was reacting.

And that was Wendy's business alone.

An older woman shuffled up the aisle toward the theater door. I moved to open it for her and held it while she made her way through. With a last glance at the stage, I followed her into the lobby, taking care to let the door close softly.

"Thank you, young man. You wouldn't happen to know where the restrooms are, would you?"

"Yes, ma'am." I pointed to the right. "They're down that way. You'll see signs as you get close. It's not too far." Should I offer to walk her there? She seemed steady enough on her feet, but maybe that was the right thing to do.

She nodded and headed off.

I frowned, then shrugged and went back to concessions.

In the kitchen, I washed my hands and resumed my post near the fryers. It didn't look like I'd missed anything. I slipped my phone out and sent Wendy a quick text. *Just caught a snippet of the play. Wren was onstage. She looks completely fine.*

I waited to see if she'd respond. She hadn't mentioned what she'd be doing tonight. It didn't take long for my phone to buzz.

Big relief! Mom said as much, but still nice to hear. How's it going?

I smiled. How was it going? I glanced around the kitchen. Everyone was just kind of hanging out, most on their phones. Typical. *We're at a slow spot. It's hot by the fryers and I don't ever want to eat a churro again.*

Maybe that wasn't completely true, but it was going to be a while for sure. I could probably expand that to include anything covered in cinnamon and sugar.

Aww. So much for my plans at Navy Pier.

My eyebrows lifted. She had plans for visiting the pier? That must mean she was considering the Chicago visit more seriously. On Tuesday, when she'd come to my place hysterical, she'd tried to pull away. In the days since, she'd made a few comments along those lines—as if she was hoping I'd agree and push her away. But that wasn't happening. I was about halfway in love with Wendy Hall, and falling fast.

I tapped a response. *If I'm there with you, I'll eat a churro.*

Her reply was almost immediate. *It's a date.*

I grinned. *It is? When am I coming to get you?*

I thought maybe I could go with you when you left.

I stared at her text. I was planning on skipping the final performance on Good Friday—Letty had grudgingly approved it since I'd made it clear that there were others who were comfortable and confident on the fryers now. It was an eleven-hour drive, ish, back home.

Is that not okay?

I bit my lip. *No, it's great. Perfect. As long as you realize*

I'M DRIVING AND PLANNED TO LEAVE ON THE THIRD. BUT I'D BE HAPPY TO ROAD TRIP WITH YOU.

SOUNDS GOOD. LESS SCARY THAN YOUR SMALL PLANE.

I chuckled and a couple of the other concessions staff looked over. "Sorry."

They all went back to what they were doing. I tapped out one more reply. *I'D STILL LIKE TO FLY YOU HOME. BUT WE CAN DISCUSS THAT. HOW LONG CAN YOU STAY IN CHICAGO?*

IT'S SPRING BREAK THE WEEK AFTER. SO TWO WEEKS? IS THAT TOO MUCH?

Considering I'd be angling to get her to want to come back and stay forever, two weeks seemed like a great start. *NOT AT ALL. I CAN'T WAIT.*

She sent back a smiley face emoji.

I grinned and clicked my phone off before tucking it back into my pocket.

The rest of the time passed uneventfully. There were a few stragglers coming out for snacks just before we closed up—of course. Then again, I'd been known to ask for a popcorn refill on my way out of the movie theater. This was basically the same thing.

When the kitchen was cleaned and everything shut down, I followed the rest of the crew out into the crisp night air. I gave a little wave as I skirted past the still-lingering clumps of theater-goers or actors who were on their way home.

It was a nice walk. I liked to walk in Chicago, too, when I had time. This was a different feel than the city. Even though it was Friday night on a college campus, it wasn't rowdy. There were small clusters of people walking around and lights were burning in windows, but Gilead completely missed the constant hum of traffic that narrated even the quietest nights in the city.

As much as I'd enjoyed the time here, I was ready to be home.

Was Wendy really going to spend two weeks in Chicago? I couldn't stop the grin that formed as a result of that idea. She'd need somewhere to stay.

I pulled out my phone and tapped my mom's contact.

She answered on the first ring. "There he is."

"Hi, Mom. Have I not called you enough?"

She laughed. "That's a loaded question. I don't think there's such thing as enough when it comes to a mom hearing from her child."

I chuckled. "Well, you're in luck. I'll be home before you know it. Just one more weekend of performances and then I'll head home around April third. Maybe the fourth if I make the trip two days."

"Really? Oh, that's wonderful. GG said you were going to be home for Easter, but I didn't want to believe it until I heard it from you."

I pulled open the door to the dorm and raised a hand in greeting to the residence director behind the desk. "Well, now you have. I'm bringing a friend up for a visit."

"Oh?" Mom paused. "Are you going to make me beg for details?"

I unlocked my door, went in, and shut and locked it behind me. "I've talked to you about Wendy. She'd like to come for two weeks."

"And?"

I dropped onto the couch and toed off my shoes. "And I really hope you like her. Do you think she could stay at your place?"

"Of course. There's plenty of room." She sighed. "Why do you enjoy vexing me?"

"I don't know, I can't help myself." I propped my feet on the coffee table. "I like her. A lot."

"Just like?"

"For now." I wasn't ready to jump into the idea of love. Not yet. I was definitely on my way in that direction, but Wendy was right that she came with baggage. And I owed it to her—and to myself—to make sure we went slow enough to be sure.

"I like how that sounds. I know whirlwind romances sound romantic, but I've always been a fan of friendship that morphs into more."

"I know. And this isn't quite that—but it's along those lines. The friendship and the more kind of developed together." That didn't make any sense when I stopped to think about it, but hopefully Mom understood.

"Hm."

"Don't hm me, Mom. I like her. I said that. I think she's the one, okay? But we're going slow."

"Because?"

Here's where it got a little tricky. Mom might be completely cool with Wendy's past. Or, she could be dismissive. I cleared my throat. "She's a widow. She lost her husband and two daughters in a car accident a little over a year ago."

Silence stretched across the call.

"Mom?"

"That's...tragic. And I guess I understand more about why you're going slow." She sighed. "If this is the woman God has for you, I'm going to love her. I hope you know that."

"I do. I know it's not what you dreamed of."

"That doesn't matter, honey. God's plans are always better. I'll look forward to meeting Wendy when you get here. And your grandmother and I will have fun entertaining her while you work."

I nodded. I wasn't going to be able to avoid spending a few days in the office when I got back. But once I got the big fires out, I could probably work my time in such a way that Wendy and I had the bulk of our days together. "Thanks. I asked her to help me redecorate."

"Oh? Well. That sounds like a grand idea. Your place has been in desperate need of a makeover since you moved in."

"She hasn't completely agreed yet. Maybe you can work on her."

"I'll see what I can do. If nothing else, it'll give us something to talk about."

"Thanks, Mom. I'll see you soon."

"Can't wait. I'm proud of you, and I love you."

"Love you, too." I ended the call and sighed. Was it okay to be nervous about bringing a woman home to meet my family? It seemed like, at my age, it shouldn't be a big deal. But I loved Mom, Grandmother, and GG. And I respected their opinions.

I really, *really*, wanted them to like Wendy.

And for Wendy to like them.

I pushed off the couch and headed into the bedroom. I wanted a shower and then maybe I'd see if Wendy wanted to do a streaming watch party from our respective homes while we drifted off to sleep.

It was the next best thing to where I hoped things would take us someday.

23

WENDY

I stared at my suitcase by the front door and bit my lip. Was I really doing this? I turned as Mom came in from my kitchen with a to-go mug in her hand.

"You're ready? You have your charging cables and toothbrush?"

I laughed as I took the mug from her and set it aside. "Yes. To all of them. You sound nervous. I thought that was my job."

"I think it's all right for us both to feel it. I'll miss you."

"It's only two weeks." And I wasn't going to mention that she and Dad were heading off to the Caymans with Scott and Whitney again tomorrow. Did Preston go to the Caribbean like Scott and his friends seemed to? Or was there another vacation spot he preferred? I made a mental note to ask him.

"I know. And we won't even be home. But this is really the first time you've gone off like this." Mom's smile wobbled around the edges. "I'm proud of you."

"You are?"

"Of course I am." Mom planted her hands on her hips. "Wendy Hall, are you really going to stand there and tell me you don't know how proud I am of you?"

I hunched my shoulders. "Maybe?"

"Oh, baby." Mom opened her arms and I stepped into them. She pressed a kiss to my forehead. "I love you. The last year has been so hard, watching you wade through your grief and not knowing how to help. But you've never once let me down."

The truth welled up in my throat and I fought against it. Mom didn't need to know. Even if she'd hinted a few weeks ago that she suspected life wasn't as picture perfect as the outward image Mark demanded, I still didn't need to crush all her perceptions. Did I?

"What is it?" Mom stepped back and searched my face.

"I was going to divorce him." I clamped my lips shut too late so instead closed my eyes so I didn't have to see the disappointment on Mom's face.

"Good."

I popped one eye open, then the other. "I'm sorry, what?"

"I said good. Your daughters wouldn't know a secret if their life depended on it. Dad and I were trying to support you and not interfere, because you didn't seem to want that. We figured you'd ask us for help. You never did. You always did try to do everything on your own. So we've just tried to keep up the pretense that we thought everything was perfect. It seemed to be what you wanted. Or needed." Mom reached for my hand. "Should we have stepped in? It's been one of our biggest regrets. The girls...maybe if we had, they'd still be with us."

I swallowed. "No. Mom you can't go down the what-if path. That's one good thing I learned in therapy. But I'm sorry I shut you out. I thought I needed to be perfect. To do it all right on my own. I'm finally realizing that's not how it's supposed to work. At all."

"At the risk of repeating myself, good."

I smiled. Maybe I was particularly slow when it came to learning lessons, but I was glad I was finally beginning to see—

and to truly believe—that I didn't have to do it on my own. That message on the grander scale was one I'd been witnessing every year my entire life with the passion play. Jesus had come to Earth to die because we *couldn't* be perfect enough without Him. So why had I thought I was an exception to that?

No idea.

"I love you, Mom. And Dad, too."

Mom chuckled. "I'll be sure to tell him you phrased it that way."

"Definitely. He'll get a kick out of it."

"What time is Preston picking you up?"

I checked my smart watch. "Should be any time now. His mom talked him out of driving the whole way in a day, so we'll stop in St. Louis."

Mom nodded. "That's what, seven hours?"

"About that. It leaves four or so for tomorrow." Technically, swinging down to St. Louis made the trip a tiny bit longer, but he'd thrown out the idea of seeing the arch and I hadn't been able to say no. I'd always planned to travel. Mark had said he wanted that, too. And then, when we were married, it all changed. Leaving Gilead to go anywhere made me want to see everything I possibly could. I was going to embrace each step of this journey.

"That sounds lovely. I don't have to remind you—"

"You absolutely do not."

Mom shook her head. "He's an attractive man. You're a beautiful woman. You like each other. You can understand a mother worries."

My face was on fire. "He hasn't even kissed me yet."

"What's wrong with him?" Mom scowled. "You've been dating a month!"

"We're going slow." I wasn't sure it had been a full month, but I didn't feel like being accused of avoiding the topic.

"That's not slow, that's glacial."

I smiled. "It's sweet. But I'm hoping when we're on his turf he'll feel a little more inclined to move in that direction."

Mom looked like she had a lecture building up, but thankfully she kept it in check because the doorbell rang.

I grabbed the knob and turned it, grinning when I saw Preston on the porch. "Hi."

"Hi. Can I get your bags?" He nodded to my suitcase and leaned in to look around. "Hi, Mrs. Hall."

"Hi Preston. Take good care of my daughter."

"Yes, ma'am. That's the plan." He turned to me. "This is it?"

I nodded. "I figured I could do laundry."

"Of course. Yeah. Mom and Grandmother never go anywhere without at least two cases." He reached for the suitcase handle. "I'll see you at the car?"

"Sounds good." I waited for him to get down the steps of the porch before turning to Mom. "Have fun in the islands. Tell Whitney I said hi."

"I will. You have fun, too. And if he drags his feet too long on the kissing front, don't be afraid to take matters into your own hands." Mom winked and stepped through the front door.

I grabbed my purse and the go-cup of coffee, glanced around one more time, checked the lock and pulled the door closed behind me. I gave the handle a twist to check that it had latched and waved to Mom as she got in her car.

I circled around to the passenger side of Preston's car and got in.

He glanced over as I settled my purse on the floor and put my cup in one of the holders. "The house will be okay?"

"Yeah. I've got a couple of people who will swing by and check on things while I'm gone. That's one of the few benefits of small-town life." I smiled and reached over my shoulder for the seat belt.

"Good. That's good." Preston started the engine and put his hand on the shifter. Then he paused, leaned across the console, and took my face in his hands. He pressed his lips to mine. My eyes drifted closed and I leaned closer. My hands came up to cover his as I lost myself in the sensation.

When he eased back, I took a deep breath.

He held my gaze, quirked a brow, and said, "Are you ready for an adventure?"

I looked into his eyes and nodded. "As long as I'm going with you."

EPILOGUE

Cooper
Christmas, the same year

"I'm not sure why we've never thought to come to the islands for Christmas before." I wiggled to adjust my position in the lounge chair on the pool deck and glanced over at Preston. "It's too bad the rest of the guys didn't make the trip."

Preston shrugged. "I'm not a big beach person, you know that. But when Scott and Whitney invited us down—and Wendy was so excited about the idea—I didn't know how to say no. I'm glad you could come."

"Especially since it meant you got to be in the same place as Wendy for more than a long weekend, I imagine." I peered over the rim of my sunglasses and waggled my eyebrows.

"Long distance relationships are hard, I will give you that. But I'm hoping to put a stop to that that before much longer."

"Yeah?" I grinned. "About time."

"There were reasons not to rush. You know that."

I did. Or most of them, at least. I suspected that maybe all the details hadn't been shared with the family. But that was okay. Everyone deserved to have some privacy. Regardless, I was glad my brother and Wendy were still together and sickeningly in love. It took some of the pressure off the rest of us. Plus, Wendy was perfect for Preston.

As if I'd summoned her with my thoughts, Wendy strode across the pool deck in her swimsuit, a brightly patterned sarong tied around her waist.

"There you all are." She sat on the side of Preston's lounge and leaned in for a long kiss.

I looked away, but not before muttering, "Get a room."

Wendy laughed. "Sorry, Coop."

"Uh-huh. Sure you are." I returned her grin. "Where's everyone else?"

"They're bringing food. Should we set up out here or do you two want to come in to fix a plate?"

"We can come in." Preston sat up and swung his legs over the other side of his lounge chair. He stood and came around to offer Wendy a hand up, then tucked her close to his side.

I shook my head and stood. We'd been eating like kings since we landed. I didn't really need another meal right now, but I also wasn't willing to pass it up. I followed behind the love-birds, trying to fight the urge to roll my eyes or make gagging noises. They really were too sweet to be believed.

In the kitchen, Mom and Grandmother were already seated at the counter with plates of food. Whitney, Wendy's sister, was fixing a plate that was probably for their son from the looks of it. Her husband, Scott, had the boy drawing at the kitchen table. Preston stood behind Wendy, his arms linked around her waist.

Mr. and Mrs. Hall came in from the garage with a bowl of ice and a box of pop.

Preston glanced around and cleared his throat. "Now that we're all here, before we dive in, I wanted to say something."

Mrs. Hall's hand flew to her mouth. A glance at Mom and Grandmother showed them leaning forward.

"Just about a year ago, GG convinced me to get in touch with her alma mater and figure out the best way for the family to set up an endowment for the students there. That first phone call on New Year's Day connected me to Wendy, and I'm so grateful to God that it did." Preston leaned down to kiss Wendy's head.

"Me, too." Wendy smiled up at him.

"Wendy, you know I love you. And I know you love me. We've managed dating long distance, but I want that to stop. Will you marry me? Move to Chicago and be a permanent part of my life?"

Wendy turned to face Preston, her eyes glistening. "Yes. Absolutely yes."

I looked away as my brother drew Wendy into his arms for a dramatic kiss. I didn't begrudge them happiness. At all. I'd enjoyed getting to know Wendy and she and Preston were a perfect fit. And after hearing about all that Wendy had gone through in her first marriage, I could appreciate the beauty of God bringing her a new start at Easter.

If I was a little jealous because Preston seemed to have it all together and I had no idea what I should be doing with my life? Well, that was a me problem.

~

More of the Swift brothers coming soon! In the mean time, if you haven't read about Wendy's sister, Whitney, you can find that story in <u>The Billionaire's Nanny</u>*.*

ACKNOWLEDGMENTS

The idea for a series set at Easter was initially Valerie Comer's. She and I (along with occasional others like Lee Tobin McClain and Lynnette Bonner) kicked around the idea for the better part of two years. We all agreed that Easter books were seriously underrepresented in the marketplace. But we were also hesitant to undertake another multi-author series.

In the end, due to life and other things, the original group of six morphed several times into the (hopefully) five authors who finished. I say hopefully, because at the time I'm writing this, it's still not clear that the final two authors will be able to get theirs written and published. Because life seems to be hitting them rather harder than usual.

It happens.

Still, I'm exceedingly grateful to Valerie Comer, Heather Gray, Deb Kastner, and Narelle Atkins for at least sticking with the project long enough to make it through the cover design phase and give us all a little bit of hope that this series could see the light of day in one form or another.

I continue to be so grateful to you - the reader - for being willing to take a chance on any words I put down on the page. It's a leap of faith by you and I will never, ever take it for granted.

Thanks, as always, to my family, for letting me take time and space to write. For being okay with tacos for dinner more than once a week some weeks, and for not minding when it's spaghetti the other nights.

Thanks also go, as ever, to my writer friends. Some days, a

Facebook message with you is the difference between running screaming and being willing to face the keyboard and try again.

Finally, first, last, and in between, my forever thanks is to Jesus. I'm grateful for salvation. For His love. For words. For the stubbornness that keeps me going some days. For the whisper of the Holy Spirit in my heart. It's my prayer that these words that I'm given will be used for His glory.

WANT A FREE BOOK?

If you enjoyed this book and would like to read another of my books for free, you can get a free e-book simply by signing up for my newsletter on my website.

OTHER BOOKS BY ELIZABETH MADDREY

Billionaire Next Door

The Billionaire's Nanny

The Billionaire's Best Friend

The Billionaire's Secret Crush

The Billionaire's Backup

The Billionaire's Teacher

The Billionaire's Wife

Postcards, A Novel

So You Want to Be a Billionaire

So You Want a Second Chance

So You Love to Hate Your Boss

So You Love Your Best Friend's Sister

So You Have My Secret Baby

So You Need a Fake Relationship

So You Forgot You Love Me

Hope Ranch Series

Hope for Christmas

Hope for Tomorrow

Hope for Love

Hope for Freedom

Hope for Family

Hope at Last

Peacock Hill Romance Series

A Heart Restored

A Heart Reclaimed

A Heart Realigned

A Heart Redirected

A Heart Rearranged

A Heart Reconsidered

Arcadia Valley Romance – Baxter Family Bakery Series

Loaves & Wishes

Muffins & Moonbeams

Cookies & Candlelight

Donuts & Daydreams

The 'Operation Romance' Series

Operation Mistletoe

Operation Valentine

Operation Fireworks

Operation Back-to-School

Prefer to read a box set? Find the whole series here.

The 'Taste of Romance' Series

A Splash of Substance

A Pinch of Promise

A Dash of Daring

A Handful of Hope

A Tidbit of Trust

Prefer to read a box set? Get the series in two parts! Box 1 and Box 2.

The 'Grant Us Grace' Series

Wisdom to Know

Courage to Change

Serenity to Accept

Pathway to Peace

Joint Venture

Prefer to read a box set? Grab the whole series here.

The 'Remnants' Series:

Faith Departed

Hope Deferred

Love Defined

Stand alone novellas

Kinsale Kisses: An Irish Romance

Luna Rosa (part of A Tuscan Legacy)

For the most recent listing of all my books, please visit my website.

ABOUT THE AUTHOR

USA Today bestselling author Elizabeth Maddrey is a semi-reformed computer geek and homeschooling mother of two who lives in the suburbs of Washington D.C. When she isn't writing, Elizabeth is a voracious consumer of books. She loves to write about Christians who struggle through their lives, dealing with sin and receiving God's grace on their way to their own romantic happily ever after.

facebook.com/ElizabethMaddrey

instagram.com/ElizabethMaddrey

amazon.com/Elizabeth-Maddrey/e/B00A11QGME

bookbub.com/authors/elizabeth-maddrey